ARIELLA'S KEEPER

DIVINITY HEALERS

MICHELLE M. PILLOW

MICHELLE M. PILLOW® - MICHELLEPILLOW.COM

Forced to stay in his home as his ward, she has no choice but to do whatever he wants. When he demands she marry his son, Ariella finds this is one order she might not mind obeying.

In Asclepius there are only two classifications of people. Doctors and Not Doctors (Sans). They are the go-to plane for anything medical. In fact, they're so focused on health it's become a bit of an obsession. Plants are encased in glass to protect people from allergens. The air is pumped full of chemicals to keep it sterile.

This is a plane teeming with germ-a-phobes.

The Playful Prince

The Bound Prince

The Rogue Prince

The Pirate Prince

Captured by a Dragon-Shifter Series

Determined Prince

Rebellious Prince

Stranded with the Cajun

Hunted by the Dragon

Mischievous Prince

Headstrong Prince

Space Lords Series

His Frost Maiden

His Fire Maiden

His Metal Maiden

His Earth Maiden

His Woodland Maiden

Qurilixen Lords Series

Dragon Prince

Marked Prince

More Coming Soon!

To learn more about the Qurilixen World series of
books and to stay up to date on the latest book list
visit www.MichellePillow.com

Divinity Warriors

Lilith Enraptured

Fighting Lady Jayne

Keeping Paige

Taking Karre

Divinity Healers

Ariella's Keeper

Seducing Cecilia

Linnea's Arrangement

To my editor, Suz.

CITY OF ASCLEPIUS, COUNTRY OF
CHIRON, DIMENSIONAL PLANE 187

THERE WAS LITTLE WORSE than being stuck in a medical dimension as the undeserving prisoner of an overbearing doctor. And, since that doctor happened to be the Medical Supreme, by all rights the most powerful man on dimensional plane 187, Ariella was even more out of luck. For who would go up against such a powerful man in order to save an off-plane woman from an alternate reality? A woman with nothing and no one to make her rescue worthwhile?

Supreme Walter didn't trap her in with chains or lock her away with iron bars. No, his plan was much simpler and much more diabolical. He had injected her with a virus, specifically engineered by him to keep her within his home and forever under his control. Her body became her jailer, the boundaries of her flesh her prison walls. She couldn't run, couldn't escape. If she wasn't so tormented by what was done to her, she might actually admire the sick perfection in which the Medical Supreme kept her.

Then again, probably not.

Only the chemical antidote he pumped into the mansion's air vents kept her alive. Sure, she had an inhaler so she could walk the grounds or for when he wished to take her out and show her off as his ward. But if she were out for longer than six hours, she'd die a horrifically painful death.

If Ariella disobeyed him, he took away her cure. If she vexed him or refused his orders, he took away her cure. If she didn't make certain the servants had his evening sustenance on the table on time, he took away her cure. If she didn't log in at least an hour of exercise a day and keep her food intake down, he took away her cure.

Yep, a definite pattern.

"And when he tires of me or demands more than I can give, he'll take away my cure," Ariella whispered, staring at her reflection in the mirror. Sometimes she barely recognized herself. It wasn't just the toning of her daily exercise, though that did take away the softness from the figure prized in her youth.

Her clothes were the height of Chiron fashion consisting of a pair of loose black slacks and a long gray shirt with a stripe of green down the front to match her eyes. She'd been forced to grow out her blonde hair, letting the waves fall down over her back. Running her finger over her lips, she watched the color stain smear only to regroup exactly where it belonged.

One of the benefits of living on one of the most medically advanced planes of existence was the constant monitoring of health. She'd never felt better in her life—unless her cure was taken away, of course. Every meal, though bland, was perfectly balanced with her body's dietary needs for the day. If she became overly stressed, one of the maids appeared to give her a shot in the neck to take the symptoms away. Her heartbeat was monitored by the mansion's central computer, as was her location.

Captive. Prisoner. No escape.

The words filtered through her mind in a constant stream, repeating over and over throughout her day. She wondered if she were to run and never come back if she'd even be allowed to die. It was possible Supreme Walter would save her and force her back, after a sufficient amount of punishment of course.

Ironically, she'd come to this dimension for a cure, but while she was getting treatment there was a rebellion on her home dimension and her family was killed. Without her father's political position, Divinity Corporation had little use in demanding the Medical Supreme send her back to her home reality. Besides, there was nothing on her home dimension to go back to but certain death. She'd be murdered the moment she appeared through the portal.

Though the viability of alternate realities was well known and accepted on her home dimensional plane, Divinity Corporation had the only known source of inter-dimensional travel technology. They were her only hope, for no one in the Chiron capitol city of Asclepius would take her word over the Medical Supreme, and Divinity was not coming to save her.

Out of the four hundred thirty-six known dimensions, Ariella had only been to three alternate realities—home, a Divinity base and this one. Each foreign dimension was like looking at a copy of her home world, if history had evolved in a different way. To a point there were many similarities. Languages were relatively similar. Some people appeared the same, but were not the same people. Certain events, like natural disasters, were shared, and the planet was still basically the same planet.

"But this is not home." She looked at the ceiling of her bedroom. The longer she stared, the smaller the great room felt. Like all places on this plane, the room was overly sterile, each surface hard and unwelcoming but for a few engraved curls and wisps decorating the edges. Marble and metal blended together with great square columns to form self-sterilizing walls. The gray and green chairs and bedding matched her clothing. By Chiron standards, it was the most lavish of places.

Swallowing nervously, she again turned her attention to the long mirror. Supreme Walter had been acting strange, becoming more possessive of her time and ordering a full array of checkups—tests that centered a little too intimately on her private regions, as if confirming she was a virgin yet again. The man was obsessed ever since he'd discovered her maidenly status at her first medical appointment. Where she came from, it wasn't such a rare thing. People were expected to wait, though she knew not everyone did.

Ariella was no fool. She knew what men wanted with their leering eyes and lustful bodies. She had seen the educational films, read the forbidden manuals, whispered girlish secrets to her now-passed sisters. She had seen the way Supreme Walter stared at her stomach and hips, as if calculating the children she would have. It left her feeling cold and empty.

"Tonight wear the new clothes I bought for you and wash your body well," he had said as she stood from the dining table. "I have put scented lotion on your dressing table. Use it. Everywhere."

Lifting her fingers, she smelled the herbal concoction on her hands. It was pleasantly sweet and a horrible omen of what was to come. If she thought it would do any good, she would jump from her second-story window. Though, the last time she tried to end her life, the mansion's security devices activated and caught her in an invisible net. Walter had not been pleased.

"If I must do this, I beg the goddesses that he should find his release quickly." Her thighs tightened, clamping together. The very idea of him coming over her naked body made her stomach ache. "Or perhaps his heart will seize before the time comes and I will be free."

Who was she kidding? The other doctors would only save him.

2

"Father." Dr. Sebastjan Walter didn't appreciate being summoned to the family mansion—even if the summons had come a month earlier to give him plenty of time to make arrangements. He had no use for the cold marble and hollow feelings that filled his childhood home. The moment he was of age with his medical degree in hand, he'd left for his first and only post—a research facility on the far side of the planet, about as far away as he could get from the social life of Asclepius and the mansion home of his Medical Supreme father.

"Sebastjan," his father acknowledged with a self-satisfied grin. The smooth, almost youthful appearance of his skin belied his years, but the calculating light in his blue eyes made up for it. He'd allowed some of his black hair to gray along the temples. People often said Sebastjan looked like the man, but for his nose that came from his late mother's side. Sebastjan didn't necessarily like hearing that. "How happy I am that you have arrived safely, son." The man looked at the screen on the wall. "If not on time."

Sebastjan followed his father's gaze to the time on the wall. He was over an hour late. "I didn't have much choice." He took a seat in front of his Walter's desk, trying to force himself to relax in the wide-cushioned chair. He hated the oversized furniture. It made him feel like a kid again, dwarfed by his father's all-consuming presence. He turned his attention back to the blank medical interface screen on the wall, wishing it were time for him to go. "Apparently, it was be here or my laboratory was going to be permanently sealed. I could have fought your shut-down order if you were to make it. My team has just come into possession of a new, very promising substance. However, I thought making an appearance would be easier."

His father's smile faded at the comment. "I had hoped you would have gotten over your childish impulses and lack of verbal control. You are a director of a research facility now, Sebastjan. Not some schoolboy running about in knickers, searching for ways to vex his father."

Impulses? Sebastjan frowned. His father considered anything contrary to what he wanted a childish impulse whether it was words or deeds.

"I asked you not to call in that favor," Sebastjan answered, irritated and growing more so by the second. "I could have made director on my own. I *preferred* to make director on my own."

"In another five years or so," the Medical Supreme quipped. "My son does not work for anyone. You are above the others of this planet. You were meant for more. Someday, you will be meant for my position. There are expectations that—"

"I don't work for anyone? So you're saying I don't have to listen to you?" Sebastjan smiled at the very idea. If only.

"What substance?" his father asked, not deigning to answer his son's rude interruption or insolent questions. "That blue mineral water we took off a visiting Divinity Corporation analyst? Your lab took point on that?"

"Yes. It's from an underground spring on a plane called Staria. I've put in a request with someone named Sans Lady Lilith for trade. Apparently, she is a Divinity liaison living amongst a race of barbarians.

I hope to obtain more." Sebastjan relaxed. Medical advancements seemed to be the only subject in which he and his father could have a decent conversation. "It stays eternally warm, even without a heat source. If we can synthesize the mineral, just think of the possibilities. Deaths by freezing will be drastically decreased. All of our mountain and deep sea expedition teams can go longer and farther."

"So you are waiting to hear from this Sans Lady Lilith?"

"Yes." Sebastjan nodded. "The Starians are making a list of what they would like in return. I should be able to get it for a few medical lasers and a handheld unit. Though she appears civilized enough, I can't imagine the barbarians knowing what to ask for beyond a few toys."

"Ah, so there is no need for you to get back to your lab right away. Wonderful. You can stay here for a couple weeks."

A couple weeks with my father? Ah, no. Make that no poppicockin way. "I can't. There is much preparation to—"

"I insist." His father stood. "I have a surprise planned, but first you must meet my ward. We call her Sans Ariella for she is without a surname. She came to us through the inter-dimensional portals.

Her father was murdered on her home plane and she has nowhere else to go."

"Another *ward*?" Sebastjan grimaced. Since his mother's death when he was a boy, his father had taken in many "wards". "I have no interest in meeting your newest lover. I am sure she's as vapid as the last twenty."

"Oh, you will want to meet Ariella. She is special." His father picked up a news reader and handed it over to him. "Very special. Her mind is unspoiled by the logic of our society. She does not think like a doctor." Walter hummed thoughtfully. "She is...innocent."

Sebastjan took the small, square, electronic unit. The front of the social pages stared back at him. He stiffened. This had to be a joke. "You're planning a wedding?"

"I believe the correct phrase would be, I *have* planned a wedding." His father grinned. "And it takes place tonight."

"I want no part in this," Sebastjan said, standing. His father placed his hand on a scanner and he heard the exterior shields lowering around the house. The lights dimmed as the orange glow from the early evening sun was blocked out. Small panels opened up on the walls and candleholders slid out. Fake candles lit, giving a soft orange glow as the shields fell into place.

"You don't have a choice. If I could do it without you, I would, but unfortunately the law requires that you be here as a willing participant when you take a wife." His father smiled and Sebastjan fell back into his chair at the look. "One call and everything you hold dear will fall down around you, or you can do this one simple thing I ask of you."

"You want me to get married to your lover?" Sebastjan had the vague impression that the ceiling would come crashing down at any moment. Out of all the orders he had been given in his life, this was the most insane. If not for the mandated medical checkups that said the Medical Supreme was fit to serve, Sebastjan would have thought his father was losing his mind. Instead, he knew the man was just calculating and manipulative. Walter would stop at nothing to force people to his will.

"She is not my lover and I command you to marry her. She is everything you need in a wife—a paragon of social values and morals, the very picture of decorum and etiquette. I have groomed her for you. She is meek and pleasant to look at..."

His father kept talking but Sebastjan barely heard a word he said. The kind of woman Walter described hardly sounded like someone he'd choose to marry. But then, he wasn't choosing. Somehow, Sebastjan had always known that his marriage would be something of a political, if not genetically based, alliance. Though, he never expected his father would outright choose for him.

Sebastjan had dated the kind of women his father wanted for him—vapid, shallow, mindless future doctors' wives. In Chiron if you weren't a doctor, you did everything to make sure you were married to one and lived your life to serve. He didn't want to be served. If he ever did marry, which wasn't the plan, it wouldn't be to someone his father would like. He wanted a woman who thought for herself, had her own work obsession and, quite frankly, left him alone so he could do his research.

Apparently, Walter didn't think his son answered fast enough, because he warned, "Consider carefully. Think of your job, your friends, your life, your inheritance, your position as a doctor. I may be your father, but I am also Medical Supreme. I can take everything away from you."

Sebastjan drew his finger over the screen, sliding the article up so he could see the announcement pictures. No surprise that the "bride" was pretty. The picture of her showed her turning toward the camera, green eyes lifting for the briefest of seconds as if to meet with his. His stomach tightened slightly at the recorded look, but he kept all emotion out of his voice and expression. "If I do this, you will promise never to meddle in my life or career again." Sebastjan threw the news reader on the desk. It landed with a hard thud. "And I want it in writing. This is the last time. After this, my life is my own."

3

ARIELLA TOOK A DEEP BREATH, stopping on her way down the stairs to look around the quiet house. An array of items from other dimensional planes decorated Walter's home, her prison. A loud cranking sound echoed as the lights grew dim. Something slid over the windows, blocking out the light. This had never happened before. Slowly she continued down, cautiously watching the darkening stone floor below. False firelight replaced sunlight. The romantic implications were not lost. Her breathing became shaky. She was always trapped, but seeing the outside light fade as the home became encased made the tomblike feelings all the more real.

"I can't," she whispered, stopping on the bottom step. "I can't do this. Don't make me."

"Ariella. Join us." Supreme Walter appeared around the corner. He smiled, but that was nothing new. He always smiled at her, like a great benefactor bestowing his grace upon those beneath him.

Beneath him.

She grimaced, pushing the thought from her brain. "I'm a little tired. Perhaps I should rest? I need to rest. I'll just go—"

Supreme Walter reached into his pocket, the action cutting off her hasty words. He took out a remote. Pressing a button once, he turned on the room's medical interface screen. Instantly, Ariella's statistics appeared, giving him every intimate detail of her body's inner workings. She refused to read the details. There was something all the more violating about being physically read. "Your lidic levels are elevated." He pushed another button, ordering medication. "I'll have the maids bring you a correcting shot. Though, you have no reason to be stressed, my dear. You should be happy. This is a great day."

Ariella gave a pained laugh. A great day? Happy? No reason to be stressed? Her entire life had become a reason to be stressed.

Supreme Walter frowned and his eyes narrowed in obvious displeasure. "I should not have to explain myself, but I will. You owe your life to me. Without me you would be on the streets, homeless, dimensionless, starved and dying if not dead already. I cured your diseased bones. I took you in. I gave you social status and grace. I did not have to do any of this, but I did out of mere generosity of spirit."

Ariella knew better than to comment.

Walter took in her silence. "Now, you owe me for that generosity. You will walk into that room and do what I tell you. You will not speak of our arrangement to anyone, under any circumstances. Tonight you will do exactly what I require." He grabbed her arm, hauling her across the front hall toward his office. There was a frenzied rush to his steps as if he were beginning to lose his patience. She'd never seen him out of sorts. He paused by his office door. "If my son suspects anything, I will not be pleased. You know what happens when I am not pleased. Now put a smile on that pretty face of yours. Good. There it is."

Ariella held her expression. She had no idea what she was walking into. Her feet dragged as she forced herself to follow him. The doors to his office slid open without him touching them. Inside, the room was cast in shadows. One of Supreme Walter's friends, Dr. Grace, waited in front of his desk holding an electronic reader. Next to him was a man she didn't recognize. The stranger's back was to her, but he was dressed in loose black pants and a long gray shirt to match hers.

"What is this?" Ariella whispered. At her words, the man in gray turned. She squinted, unable to see his face in the shadows. She studied his silhouette, seeing the stiff way he carried himself. Broad shoulders led to a trim waist. Firelight danced on black hair cut a little long for Asclepius' style. It curled slightly at his ears. She narrowed her eyes, stepping closer, trying to see his face.

"Sans Ariella," Dr. Grace said. He was a short man whose body was withered with age and yet he moved with ease.

"Doctor?" Ariella continued forward, remembering the Supreme's order to smile. If the expression looked strained, none of the men let on or perhaps they didn't care.

"Please offer your hand to Dr. Walter as a sign of your intent to join with him," Grace said.

Ariella inhaled sharply. She looked at the Medical Supreme. The man eyed her coolly, expectantly.

Grace continued, "Dr. Sebastjan Walter. Take Sans Ariella's hand as a sign of your acceptance of her intention before the witness of myself and your father."

Sebastjan? Supreme Walter motioned Ariella to obey. She turned to the stranger, to Sebastjan, to her keeper's son. Her hand shook as she lifted it, confused. Intention? The man hesitated briefly before lifting his hand to clasp hers. He held her firmly in his large, warm palm and seemed so steady against her uncertainty.

"Do they have your blessing, Medical Supreme?" Grace leaned to look around the hand-holding couple.

"They do," Supreme Walter said.

"Congratulations, Dr. and Sans Sebastjan Walter." Grace held up his reader and pressed a button. Light flashed as he took the new couple's picture. Sebastjan's face lit for the briefest second. It was enough for her to see the fullness of his lips and the hard set of his eyes.

"I'm sorry," Ariella said. "Did he call me...?"

"Wife," Sebastjan said. His voice was low and dispassionate. His hand tightened on hers. That one word caused chills to work over her body.

"Wife?" she repeated.

"Congratulations," Supreme Walter said. "Go on upstairs. Sebastjan, your room is ready. I expect you both down tomorrow morning to confirm the union and to receive your guests." To Dr. Grace, he added, "Once you have finished your report to the statistical office, why don't you join me for a drink?"

"I'm sending them the photographic evidence and confirmation now," Grace answered, tapping on his reader as he followed behind the Medical Supreme. "All I need is your signature and it's done."

The candle lights flickered as the scraping sounded once more. Light was slowly let in from outside as the thick shutters lifted. It had gotten darker out during her wedding. Wedding. The word reverberated in her head as if whispered from far away. Ariella didn't move as she watched the light shine on her husband's face. Husband. Out of all the ways she expected this day to end, married to the Supreme's son wasn't one of them.

"What does this mean now?" she wondered, only realizing afterwards that the words were said out loud.

Blue eyes met hers, their depths stormy and discontented. He searched her face, not smiling as he did so. Was he displeased with her? With the marriage? Then why did he agree? Is that why Supreme Walter turned down the lights so his son wouldn't see? Or so his son wouldn't try to jump out of the window? He didn't let go of her, even when she lightly tugged her hand.

He was handsome, even by a medical plane's standards where everyone had surgical help if they so needed. Full lips and a proud nose and those tormented eyes. He blinked and his expression blanked. "Come on then."

He finally let go of her and she flexed her aching hand, realizing how tightly he'd been holding on to her. Sebastjan didn't look at her as he walked from the room. A moment's relief flooded her as she realized she'd been wrong. She wasn't going to have to give herself to Supreme Walter. The relief was short-lived. She might not have to give herself to her keeper, but it appeared as if she would be expected to give herself to his son.

4

SEBASTJAN FLEXED HIS HAND, not bothering to turn and look at the woman behind him. He knew she would follow. She had agreed to marry him, hadn't she? Him, a stranger to her. Undoubtedly the lure of his position in Chiron society was enough for her. She, the rich doctor's wife.

It didn't matter now. He had his agreement. One wife in exchange for freedom in all other matters. It was a small price to pay. She was pretty and her body would satisfy his lusts as well as any other. And if it didn't, he'd keep a mistress as a lover and this woman in some home as a wife. Perhaps he'd get his father to buy the mansion next door. Let Ariella and Walter enjoy each other's society while he continued on as he pleased without their interference.

Despite himself, he felt his body stir as he took the stairs to his room. How long had it been? Weeks? No, more than a month since he'd been with a woman—Dr. Candra Sunn when he visited her arctic facility to arrange an ice mineral transport six weeks ago. She'd been more than eager to have an out-of-facility man in her bed. Merely hours after meeting her, she'd been on her knees with his cock in her mouth. By her skill, it was a service she provided men often. No wonder so many of the male underlings at the arctic facility walked around with smiles on their face.

Sebastjan coughed lightly at the erotic notion as he pictured this woman doing the same. Well, not to the whole male population of an arctic facility, but definitely to him. Actually, he found the idea of her serving him drinks more probable than her serving his carnal appetites. It didn't matter. Even if the sex was bad, it would happen.

Keeping his head held high and his shoulders back, he turned as he reached the top of the stairs, going down the long hallway that would lead him to his old rooms. Medical screens switched on as he passed, automatically monitoring the beat of his heart. He felt lasers trying to scan him, but he kept walking.

"What now?" Ariella asked. Her soft voice sounded so uncertain. He supposed he could speak to her, placate her somehow, but out of the two of them she was the willing spouse.

"I think you know. We finish what was started." He opened his bedroom door and stepped aside, letting her enter first. She moved inside, standing close to the wall. Sebastjan closed the door and automatically punched the keys on the panel next to it. The lights dimmed and the fireplace lit. Shades slid into place to block the evening light. He reached for the button on his shoulder, unfastening it.

Sebastjan pulled his long shirt over his head. Her breathing became labored and he glanced at her. She hadn't moved. He stopped short of unbuttoning his pants. "There is no reason to be nervous."

"Are we really...?" She glanced around the room, swayed but didn't move.

Sebastjan again reached for his waistband, but something in her expression made him hesitate. Instead he sat down on the bed. At first the mattress was stiff but soon it began to mold around his ass, conforming to his body. Unbuttoning his boots, he kicked them aside. "We both understand what this match is. You know what reasons you have and I get what I need."

5

ARIELLA TRIED NOT to stare at Sebastjan's chest. She knew what he expected but suddenly all the knowledge she had of carnal activities left her and she couldn't think. Warmth curled inside her, creeping over her belly and throughout her limbs. She found herself breathing deeply. Her hands shook. As he rolled onto his back, she took a step forward. It would be so easy to reach out and touch him, glide her fingers over the ridges of muscles.

You know what reasons you have and I get what I need.

This is what Supreme Walter had been grooming her for. She glanced at the ceiling, thinking of her cure floating in the air. There was nowhere to run. Should she beg Sebastjan to let her go? Was he different than his father? Would he give her freedom? Would he give her a cure? Or would he keep her like some living doll, trapped in his home to smile for his guests and pass out drinks at parties?

The goddesses taught her people that, once married, what happened between a man and woman was all right. She found herself walking toward him. "Your father hasn't said much regarding you."

"I'm surprised," Sebastjan answered, giving her a slight frown. He rolled up on the bed. The action brought him to sit before her. She stiffened as he reached to touch a strand of her blonde hair. "Since I am the reason he's brought you here. Didn't you care who you were going to marry?"

"I..." Ariella closed her mouth and glanced around the room. She couldn't speak ill of the Medical Supreme. "I was sick. I was sent here to the Medical Supreme so that I could be cured."

"Ah." His hand dropped. "So that is how he found you."

"I'm healthy now," Ariella quickly asserted, wondering why she felt disappointment at his withdraw.

Healthy for the most part.

"So I see." He motioned to the monitor on the wall. Ariella didn't realize it had come on, showing both of their vitals. "Shall we begin? Had I known a wedding was required of me, I wouldn't have stayed up working all of last night."

Ariella wasn't sure how to begin, so merely stood before him. He lifted his hand, again, picking up the strand of hair. He rubbed it between his fingers, as if the task was the most important in the world.

An animalistic vitality radiated off him, so much so that she had to wonder at his restraint. There was no hesitation in him, not like inside her. He didn't fear her, or this, wasn't uncertain about what to do. He dropped the lock of hair and he let his fingers brush over the top of her breast. An instant heat stung her flesh at the light touch. Her nipple tightened and her breathing deepened.

The orange fake firelight cast his features in hard contrast. He watched his fingers, taking his time as he brushed the back of his hand over her breasts. Even through the clothing, she could feel the small caress. Heat seemed to radiate from him, surrounding her, drawing her closer.

His blue eyes rose to meet hers and she held her breath. He lifted his hand to her shoulder, unbuttoning her tunic. Following the stripe, he deftly unfastened the hidden buttons until he made just enough room to reach inside. Fingers swept beneath the material, meeting flesh. This time, when he rubbed over her chest she felt the full press of his touch.

Ariella's lips parted and she inhaled a shaky breath. His opposite hand lifted to her hip, rubbing it as he worked her tunic up. He massaged her breast and hip at the same time. Fingers slid around to her back, drawing her closer.

Sebastjan unfastened a few more buttons. The front panel of the shirt fell open, exposing her breast to his eyes. He pressed his thumb to the hard nipple.

"You're trembling," he whispered. "I won't hurt you. There is no reason to be nervous."

Both hands found the flesh at the small of her back. They slid beneath her loose pants, curving along her ass cheeks. He pulled her to him and opened his mouth. A light moan escaped him as he kissed her ripe nipple.

Ariella couldn't move. She stared at his lips on her, his bronzed skin close to her paler body. His lips parted, surrounding the sensitive bud. His moan deepened as did his kiss. Soon he was sucking on her breast, pulling it deep into his mouth. Teeth bit lightly, forcing a hard jerk of surprise from her body. She swayed on her feet, feeling lightheaded.

"Mm, your breast is so soft." His tongue boldly

flicked the wet nipple. "I wonder what else is soft." He grinned, a predatory look if she'd ever seen one. "And wet."

He edged closer still, bracing his feet on the floor as he parted his legs. She glanced down, seeing the hard protrusion straining between his thighs. The dim light cast shadows so it was impossible to see the size, only the strain.

Instantly all her focus went from her breast to her thighs. A deep ache radiated from her pussy and she did feel damp there. His hands massaged her ass, rubbing deeply, pulling her cheeks apart little by little as they moved lower and around. He groaned, jerking her forward so her thighs hit the side of the bed. This time, she pressed her breast into him and he sucked it deep. His hips rocked forward, bumping lightly against her. The teasing brush of his hidden cock caught her by surprise and she jerked back. Her breast left the suction of his mouth with a loud *swack!*

"I didn't think I'd be so eager," he admitted. "It's been awhile for me."

She merely nodded, not knowing how to respond.

"I'm being greedy and doing all the exploring," he continued. "It's your turn. Go ahead. Touch me."

Despite his words, he didn't let go of her ass. Ariella looked down at her breast and wondered if she should cover up first.

Before she could decide, he insisted, "Go ahead. Touch me."

She did. Ariella placed her hand on his strong shoulders. Heat radiated from beneath her fingers, curling through her like a liquid fire to drug her senses. She breathed deeply, detecting his masculine scent. Smooth, hard muscles formed delectable chest and arms.

"Let's get this off you." Sebastjan let go of her ass and reached for her shirtfront. He pulled at the front panels, forcing it open. Buttons fell on the floor as he pushed the material off her shoulders. "Much better." He urged the sleeves off her arms and then tossed the shirt aside.

As his mouth began exploring the newly exposed breast, she ran her fingers into his silky hair. The dark strands pulled between her fingers. Groaning, he jerked her pants down her hips. They slithered to her feet.

"I said, touch me," he commanded, more forceful now as his breath came in heavy pants. He grabbed her by the wrist and brought her hand down to his stomach. Not letting go, he pulled the waistband forward, away from his cock, and shoved her hand down onto him. Swearing, he uttered, "Ah, *apolloa!*"

Ariella kept her hand against him. The firm, smooth shaft was like nothing she'd ever felt before.

"I didn't think I'd be so..." His eyes roamed freely over her naked body. "You're very beautiful." He pushed up from the bed and slid his pants from his hips. Kicking lightly, he worked them off his legs.

He wrapped his hand around hers, urging it to move. His fingers tightened, forcing hers to as well. When she learned the rhythm he liked, he let go. Sebastjan groaned, a low, completely sexual sound. He palmed her breasts, appearing fascinated with them as she leaned over.

Fingers skimmed up the side of her neck and dipped into her hair. He pulled lightly at the back of her head. Ariella's eyes widened as he tried to guide her head down.

"Mm, let's see what you can do," he murmured, pushing harder, insistently.

The low words washed over her and a scene from the forbidden manuals flashed through her thoughts. He wanted her to do *that?*

He put his hand on his cock, guiding it toward her lips. She gasped, placing her hands on his thighs for support as she leaned over his lap. The tip of his shaft slid past her lips.

Sebastjan groaned. "Suck me. That's it. That's what I like."

No man had ever dared to say such a thing. Maybe it was the sound of his voice, both pleading and insistent. Maybe it was the taste of him, or the smell, or the way his hand pressed downward. Ariella found herself obeying, letting her knees bend so she could find a better position.

He fell back on the bed, holding her head with both hands. Ariella felt powerful. She clutched his thighs, digging her nails into them as she tentatively took him deeper between her lips. Closing her eyes, she refused to think of the ramifications of her actions.

Sebastjan pressed his hips up as he pushed down, trying to force himself deeper. The warm, salty essence of him filled her mouth. She licked along the shaft, exploring the length. Her fingers slid to his cock, touching everywhere—his balls, his hips, the secret place at the base of his shaft.

"Ah, that's what I like," he moaned. His movements became jagged and frantic. Suddenly, he tensed, finding release. The taste of him filled her mouth and she swallowed. His hands fell to the side, letting her go. She pushed up, curious to see his face. He was breathing hard. Narrowed eyes stared at her. "You will make a very fine wife."

Heat warmed her cheeks as she tried, unsuccessfully, not to blush. He grabbed hold of her hips and flipped her around on the bed. She gasped, hitting the mattress. Her hands landed over her head.

His hands and knees anchored her down, trapping her to the bed. He licked his lips, his eyes roaming over her chest. Sebastjan worked his knees between hers, parting her bare thighs.

Ariella stiffened, unable to catch her breath. There was no question as to who was in control now. He ran his hand over her leg, openly exploring her with his eyes.

She wiggled beneath him, drawing her arms down to her sides. Ariella felt exposed, unsure. Sebastjan began at her neck, caressing her throat, her shoulder, each breast and nipple. Lips followed behind, continuing lower as he discovered her ribs, stomach and hips. Each time she tried to move her hands to stop him, he brushed them aside, continuing on.

As he kissed along her hip, she clamped her legs tight against his head. He didn't seem to notice. His lips moved against her thigh, closer, achingly closer to her sex. With a moan, he pressed his open mouth against her pussy. He licked hard, moaning while he did so. She pushed up on the bed, only to find his hand pressing her back down.

Heat exploded between her thighs, sending shivers of pleasure over her. He twirled his tongue, testing her, tasting her, tormenting her. As her whole body jerked, he glided over her. His hips instantly found their place between her thighs. The thick head of his cock brushed her sex. With a groan, he angled himself to her.

Ariella opened her mouth to speak, unsure what she wanted to say. She squirmed as he thrust. The tip of his cock slid inside, stretching her with its insistent push. Sebastjan groaned, his hips jerking.

Pleasure-pain erupted at the intimate contact. She gripped the bedding at her sides. He worked his hips, moving forward, pressing deeper and deeper until he'd conquered her with every inch of his arousal.

Almost breathless, he asked, "Mm, you're so tight —did you have a procedure done?"

"I..." she mumbled, "no."

Sebastjan moved in tiny circles, staying deep as he stretched her to fit him. "You must have. I don't mind.

I find I quite enjoy the experience. It makes me want to..." He groaned, pulling out and thrusting forward. "Mm, I want to pound into you." He withdrew and thrust, hard and sure. She clamped her legs against his hips. His claiming hurt, but there was a curious pleasure there too. "Ah, you're so wet and hot and tight. Relax your legs. I want to fuck you hard. I have to..."

"I..." she managed weakly. She touched his arms. The fullness of him rubbed her in a way she'd never imagined possible.

Sebastjan's cock slid in and out. He pushed back on his hands. "That's it. So good. So, uh, good. I don't want to stop. I can't stop."

With each tattered confession he began to quicken his pace until she found her body being bounced on the bed with the driving force. She began to move in rhythm with him. A light sigh escaped her and wondrous sensations filled her, building toward something she couldn't quite reach.

Sebastjan jerked violently with release before collapsing against her. Eyes wide, Ariella stared at the ceiling. He rolled next to her, his hand resting on her thigh. The light brush of his fingers caused her leg to jerk.

"You are very quiet." He rolled onto his side next

to her and she saw him squinting in the dim light. "Did you not...?"

"I, ah..."

His hand moved between her legs and he leaned close to her ear. The heat of his breath fanned over her cheek. He drew his fingers to her sex. "Let it never be said I am a greedy man."

Fingers stroked her sex, continuing where his body had left off. His thumb encircled her clit, rubbing lightly as he thrust a finger into her. He worked his hand against her, rebuilding her pleasure.

Teeth grazed the lobe of her ear. "Mm, there it is. You like when I do this, don't you?" He pressed his finger inside her, causing her body to tense and release. His words were a low whisper, as if telling her a secret even though they were alone in the room. "I can hear it in the way your breath catches." He did it again, pressing and releasing his finger inside her.

Ariella bit her lip and moaned. The sensations burst through her, spilling over her entire body. She trembled, sighed, tensed. Her mouth opened and she turned toward him. He still spoke, but she couldn't understand what he was saying. Blood rushed in her ears. His lips moved against hers and she realized he'd stopped speaking and was instead kissing her. The slow passion in the light brush of his lips made her feel weak. Or perhaps it was the aftermath of tremors dying and calming inside her.

"I suppose if we have nothing else in our marriage, there is that," he said against her mouth. He rolled onto his back, closing his eyes.

Ariella tugged at the blankets to cover herself. She watched Sebastjan's face. A small smile curled the corner of his mouth, but he didn't look at her again. Even as her heart slowed and her breathing regulated, she could barely gather a thought in her head beyond, "Oh."

6

SEBASTJAN LEFT HIS NEW "WIFE" asleep as he left his room to face his father. Despite his desire to dislike the choice his father had forced upon him, he found his step lighter than it had been in weeks. Though a little quiet, and with what he could only assume was shyness due to the newness of their situation, Ariella was quite sweet. She tasted like decadence and looked like the model of medical perfection. He'd seen the way her eyes took in everything around her, the depths of them filled with an astuteness not said with words. It made him wonder what secrets she held, what mysteries.

"Where is she?" Supreme Walter asked his son as soon as Sebastjan sat down at the long, narrow, metal table for his morning sustenance.

"Sleeping," Sebastjan answered drolly. "Would you like me to wake her for your inquisition?"

"Why? Is there a reason I should need to question her?" His father began to stand up, his brow knitting just as it did before a long lecture.

"Not that I would know," Sebastjan said. Had he been in the mood, he would have tormented the man, stringing him along with his worry. But somehow, discussing the completion of his marriage with his overbearing father didn't seem like a topic for...well, for *ever*.

"Ah, good!" His father clapped his hands. "I see I did very well grooming her for you. You will not be disappointed. She's a perfect societal gem—meek, controllable, not like your willful mother before she died. Ariella will be perfect for this family, and with the unique genetics from her plane, she will give you magnificent children—beautiful, physically perfect, strong, smart." Then grinning, he said knowingly, "And there is nothing like untouched, trainable fruit, eh?"

Sebastjan frowned, eyeing the bowl of cream-colored gruel set before him by a maid. "Untouched fruit?"

"If you insist on being indelicate," his father

scolded, "then I suppose you'd say there is nothing like a pure woman untouched by man."

Sebastjan's frown deepened and he refused to eat. Out of the two men in the room, he was hardly the indelicate one. Standing, he said, "Excuse me."

"I expect you to greet your guests!" the Medical Supreme yelled behind him as Sebastjan hurried to go back upstairs. "This match will be made official!"

Coming to his chambers, he went inside. Ariella stood in the middle of the room, concentrating on her buttons. At his entrance, she glanced up. Sebastjan didn't go to her, instead choosing to stare. Hair tumbled around her shoulders, messy from the night's sleep. Wide eyes watched him, seeming to grow wider with each passing second of silence.

"Is it true?" Sebastjan managed, well aware that his voice sounded faint.

She furrowed her brow and carefully asked, "You mean to ask if we are truly married?"

Sebastjan took a step forward, noticing how she took an involuntary step back. "Why didn't you stop me? Why didn't you say anything?"

She paled. "Your father warned me never to speak of it. I wasn't sure how you would react if you discovered the truth or if you already knew. I couldn't trust that you would do the right thing. I still don't know if..."

"Of all the meddling," he muttered. Then, going to her, he touched her cheek and forced her eyes to meet his. "You should have told me you were untouched. I would not have acted... Women on this plane are not...I didn't even think that you would be."

"Untouched? Oh, you mean..." She laughed nervously and began picking at her buttons. "I, um, it is fine. The goddesses say that with a husband is when a woman must—"

"Goddesses?" Sebastjan tried to keep the superiority out of his tone, but the confession took him by surprise. The woman clearly had primitive beliefs. His people had abandoned such thinking for the logic of science and the tangibility of facts.

"The guiding spirits," she answered. "My family served in their house."

"Ah. I see." He let her go, moving to sit on the bed. She continued to pull at her buttons, her fingers fumbling. He wondered if he made her nervous. "How did you come to be on this plane?"

"Divinity Corporation's inter-dimensional portal."

"I assumed that much since they have control of all of the portals. I meant why did they bring you?"

"I was sick and needed medical attention. My father was a political official, a very important man. Divinity Corporation wished to please him. They brought me here for a cure. When my family was murdered, they left me here for my safety. You father took me in as his ward."

"How altruistic of him," Sebastjan mumbled sarcastically. "Undoubtedly he found something in your genetics that would make you highly compatible to mine. Medical Supreme Walter only thinks of himself and the continuation of his legacy."

The overhead air-filtering sterilizer turned on, misting the room with its light fragrance. Ariella looked up and breathed deeply several times. After a few seconds, she turned back to her task, fastening her clothes with steadier hands. Finishing, she turned her full attention to him. "I need to get back to my chambers. I can't greet your guests looking like this."

Sebastjan let her leave, despite his urge to draw her back to his bed. He couldn't touch her, not after what he'd learned. Women on his plane were not shy when it came to sex, and often by the time they were well into adulthood, they had experience. Adult virgins were practically a myth. He'd never even considered meeting one, let alone marrying one. When he'd come back up and looked at her face, he remembered the hesitance he'd taken for shyness, he wanted to kick himself. He should have seen it. He should have known. She should have told him.

46

7

ARIELLA RACED TOWARD HER CHAMBERS, feeling physically stronger now that she had her medicine. She'd almost made a big mistake. She'd almost told Sebastjan about her forced illness. By the stricken look on his face when he walked into the room, she'd just assumed he'd been told about her entrapment. Instead, he was worried about her lost virginity.

The door slid up automatically as she neared. Once inside her chambers, she took a deep breath. She barely had time to process what had happened—the wedding, the wedding night, a husband—when a maid walked in holding a syringe.

"Sans Ariella," the maid said, "your lidic levels are high and your plytomikin and homytobin levels are low. I've been instructed to—"

"I know," Ariella grumbled, pulling her hair aside and tilting her head. The maid injected medicine into her in the neck. She didn't need the long explanation that came with her shots—half of which she didn't have the background to understand. If she didn't take them willingly, they'd be forced on her by Chiron's medical laws.

"There is a little extra in there to help you smile for your guests," the maid added, "and to take away any pain."

"Pain?" Ariella repeated before noticing the soreness between her thighs lessened. After a lifetime of chronic pain from her bones, she didn't even think twice of a little sexual discomfort. "Oh, never mind. Thank you for the shot."

8

THE FINEST OF Asclepius society filtered past the newlyweds' receiving line. Ariella felt herself smiling and nodding politely at each individual doctor. After some time in Asclepius, she recognized many of them. Women in fine-cut cotton and linen clothing intermingled with the dignified men. The soft sound of laughter and muted amusements created a constant background to the "thank you for coming" and "it is so kind of you to say" phrases she was forced to repeat like a trained animal.

Many of the guests looked at her with vacant eyes, seeing past her as if she were unimportant. The only exception was a few of the men. She didn't need a lifetime of sexual experience to know what they were thinking about. In fact, she overheard one of them offer to buy her from the Medical Supreme. The exact words were "I would be most honored to give the darling woman a place in my home, if you would be so good as to part with her" to which Walter answered, "Not this one. Not this time. She is not like the others."

"Congratulations, Dr. and Sans Sebastjan Walter," a woman said, looking down her hooked nose at the new bride. Ariella couldn't remember her name, but she'd talked to her often. The woman's disapproving demeanor never changed. Taking the offered gift, Ariella handed it over to the waiting maid to be set on the mountainous pile behind her.

"It is so kind of you to say," Ariella said politely.

"Thankfully it is almost over. I abhor these events," Sebastjan whispered in her ear. She glanced at him, surprised. It was the first thing he'd said to her in nearly three hours of standing in the front hall.

"Congratulations, Dr. and Sans Sebastjan Walter."

Ariella glanced away from her husband, about to answer when Sebastjan laughed and said, "Dr. Fauchet, how good of you to come."

"How could I not?" Dr. Fauchet answered. He had an easy smile with lively brown eyes that seemed to laugh at some sort of private joke.

"Couldn't miss my reception?" Sebastjan asked.

"I couldn't miss the Medical Supreme's summons," Fauchet corrected. "You didn't think everyone was here to see you, did you?"

Ariella gave a short burst of laughter in surprise at the insolent joke.

Fauchet winked at her but continued talking to Sebastjan. "Apparently, I am to host two off-plane dignitaries coming here to learn our secrets. However," he turned his full attention to Ariella, "while I am here..."

"Sans Ariella," Sebastjan introduced, "my childhood playmate and local lawbreaker—"

"That is distinguished gentleman and dignitary host," Fauchet corrected.

"Dr. Gerard Fauchet," Sebastjan finished.

"A great pleasure," Gerard said, his playful eyes studying her face. "And it was only one tiny law fourteen years ago. There was a medication mishap, it was hot and it was only the male chairmen who complained about my nakedness. I swear I am a reformed man." Ariella laughed again before catching herself. She couldn't help it. The man was just too likeable. Sebastjan cleared his throat. Gerard chuckled, not showing a single second of remorse at having been caught flirting with the new bride.

Leaning in to Ariella, he whispered, "An even greater pleasure to see you've managed to make Sebastjan jealous over you."

Ariella blushed. Sebastjan frowned at them. Gerard bowed his head and moved on.

"What? No present?" Sebastjan mumbled after him. Gerard laughed, but didn't turn back around. "What did he say to you?"

Ariella didn't answer as another guest came to offer her congratulations.

When the woman passed by, he repeated, "What did Fauchet say?"

"He said he was trying to make you jealous," Ariella answered, hiding the first genuine smile that day.

"He always did have a strange sense of humor." Sebastjan stiffly turned back to their guests.

9

Five hours. That's how long it took the procession of his father's guests to pass through the hall. Thousands of presents stacked behind them, each one demanding to be opened, each one demanding a thank-you message to be delivered.

Sebastjan grimaced. Ariella hadn't spoken to him since Gerard whispered in her ear. He liked Dr. Fauchet well enough, but didn't appreciate the fact the man made his bride blush, or that he'd winked at her on his way out of the house. "It will take us ten hours just to deliver a personal message to each gift and another thirty days to discreetly throw half of them into the incinerator."

"I'll have the maids go through them and make us a list. Perhaps a few generic messages will suffice for the bulk of them." Ariella lifted her hand, suppressing a yawn.

The Medical Supreme said farewell to the last guest. Before he could turn to them, Ariella had turned to the stairs and was walking toward the bedrooms.

"Ariella, won't you join us?" his father asked.

"I should begin organizing the gifts," she answered, stiffly turning. Sebastjan watched her carefully, noting how her eyes didn't look directly at the Medical Supreme. He had a feeling it was more than respect that kept her from the man's company. "I wouldn't want to be remiss in my duties and you have so very many friends."

"Of course," Supreme Walter agreed. "Very well."

Ariella glanced at Sebastjan, briefly meeting his eyes before turning to rush away. He wasn't sure whether to be frightened or amused by her quick handling of his father. As he'd suspected before, the woman appeared to be much smarter than the pleasant expression on her face would have people believe.

"I told you, societal perfection," his father said. "She knows her duty."

Or perhaps her reaction was merely societal training.

Sebastjan watched his father walk away. There was more going on here than he'd been told. He'd bet his medical license on it.

ARIELLA WAITED for her husband to come to her and rescue her from the endless opening of packages. She was obliged to watch, even if she didn't do the unwrapping herself. Over a dozen maids worked, several opening, others carting out the garbage to be picked up for incineration, another keeping record. Fine cotton scarves, marble figurines, linen robes, money—all of it beautiful and elegant and rich. But Ariella knew it to be more of a testament to her father-by-marriage and her husband than to herself.

Looking at the door, she willed Sebastjan to come for her. He didn't and she was not saved from her duty.

"From Dr. Darcin, an urn," one of the maids announced.

Ariella sighed, turning her attention from the door. She folded her hands in her lap and nodded her head in acknowledgment.

It took two and a half days to go through the gifts, another to record the messages necessary, two seconds to send them all out, and still another day to have them packaged and sent to Sebastjan's home at a faraway research facility. Just the idea of that facility gave Ariella cause for excitement. Finally, she would be free of her mansion prison.

Only one thing worried her. Sebastjan had not come to her as he had their wedding night. He was polite when they spoke, let her walk through doorways first and even made her laugh a few times. But she always felt as if he was watching her, waiting, searching, wondering. Several times she wanted to ask him what he was thinking, but refrained. Her favorite part of the day came when they were alone outside in the garden for her after-noon walk. Though glass containers covered all of the greenery, the air was fresh and the company handsome.

"This was my mother's favorite plant," he said, pointing at a small leafy bush. "She used to say it was the sturdiest of plants, the quiet ones, that truly made the garden. They were the ones you could depend on."

"She sounds like a wise woman," Ariella had answered.

"She used to sneak me into the garden boxes to touch the trees. My father found out and that is why all the doors now have locks. My mother hated my father and he hated her because he could not control her."

"But I am sure she loved you if she wished for you to see nature," Ariella assured him.

He didn't look comforted. "She was committed to five weeks in a mental care facility for having tried to kill me with plant allergens. She was not the same when she returned."

Ariella had no answers for that.

Each night, as she lay in bed, Ariella thought of what had happened between them on the wedding night. When he touched her, her skin had been on fire. She wanted to feel the flames again, the tense rise and trembling fall.

It was with that thought she slipped from her chambers into the dimness of the hall. Her feet whispered over the stone. The wall monitors detected her, turning on to light her way as they let her know her heart was racing a little too fast and her breathing had become hitched.

Coming to Sebastjan's door, she tried to hesitate and catch her breath, but the sensors didn't give her a chance. The door opened automatically, like a veil passing over her vision to reveal his bed. Her eyes found him easily in the dim light. He lay on his side, his back to her, bare, strong. The long line of his spine led from the shock of black hair to the tight curve of his ass.

"Sebastjan?" she whispered to see if he would awaken. He stirred, slowly coming around to look at her with sleepy blue eyes. Ariella tugged at the string holding her new robe closed. The wedding gift slithered off her shoulders. Sebastjan instantly pushed up, his gaze going to her naked breasts. Light caressed his naked flesh, contrasting the hard lines of his muscles. The limp member between his thighs stirred, straightening with interest.

Ariella had thought of this moment a lot, of what

she would do and say. Words failed her and she found it hard to move when he looked at her with those smoldering eyes. She slowly stepped toward the bed. Her knee hit the mattress. Sebastjan didn't move.

"Sans Ariella," he said, the tone like an acknowledgement, but his look made it feel more like a game.

"Doctor," she answered, her voice not as strong as she would have liked. She lifted her knee, placing it on the bed to slowly climb on.

"How may I be of service?" he inquired.

Ariella leaned forward and lifted her second leg onto the bed. "I thought I might be of service to you." She felt heat rising over her features but didn't back away. She sat back on her legs. Ariella's flesh tingled and she felt the gathering moisture between her thighs. "You have not been to see me and I thought perhaps..." Her voice failed.

His breathing visibly deepened and his member lifted and firmed. He lay back on the bed. "After..." he paused, studying her, "after our wedding night I thought it best to give you space."

"Space?"

"To wait for you to come to me. I know that I did not behave, that I did not take care of you as I should have. Had I known you were a maiden, I would have been...better."

"Better? You mean the pleasure we felt could be better?" She arched a brow in surprise. His lips parted, but no sound came out. Ariella blushed. "That did not come out right. It was too forward. That is not how I meant to say..."

"Oh? What did you have in mind?"

She opened her mouth, but couldn't think of anything clever to say.

"An examination, perhaps?" he prompted, rolling slowly onto his stomach. "With your consent, of course."

It took her a moment to realize he meant for her to play the doctor and he her patient. She smiled, nodded and reached to touch him. Shaking fingers met warm, hard flesh. She followed the length of his back, pressing along his spine. Mesmerized, she cupped his ass, massaging the cheeks. He groaned, his hips flexing into the bed. Ariella explored his legs before coming back to his hips. Every time she worked her fingers, he groaned and thrust his arousal into the bed.

"Mmm." He turned back around, faster than before, to rest on his back.

She drew her hand over his chest, following the

valleys of his muscles. He bit his lip and closed his eyes. She traced her way down the center of his stomach, following the dark trail of hair leading to his cock. Before reaching the imposing shaft, she changed course, moving back up to his neck.

Ariella touched his silky black hair, caressed his cheek and traced his firm lips. He opened his mouth, sucking her fingers against his tongue. He moaned, loud and deep.

"I ache for you," he whispered seconds before he opened his eyes in surprise, as if he hadn't meant to speak.

"Would you like me to relieve that ache?" she asked, wrapping her fingers around his cock.

Sebastjan reached for her breasts, massaging them in his palms. "Very much."

He urged her to come over him. She let go of his shaft, moving to straddle his thighs. He caressed everywhere he could reach, letting her take the lead. Ariella rubbed her sex against him, getting used to the feel. When she didn't move to take him inside her, he lifted her up by the hips and flipped her onto her back. He threaded his legs between hers, parting her thighs.

Then his lips met hers, sweet and easy. Gentleness poured into her from that kiss. It took her by surprise. Against her mouth, he whispered, "You set the pace. I will do it however you wish. I don't want to hurt you."

His cock brushed against her pussy. He took her slowly, groaning as he rocked into her. Sebastjan continued to kiss her, tracing her lips with his tongue, distracting her senses. Her eyes drifted closed. She held onto his neck, kneading the muscles she found there. He took her in shallow thrusts, his hips working in small circles. Despite his offer, Ariella simply enjoyed the pace he set, letting him slide in and out. It was unlike anything she'd ever experienced.

Tension built and she eagerly awaited the finale. The excitement made her pant into his mouth. When he thrust, she pushed up harder than before and was rewarded with a jolt of sensations. And then it happened, a complete explosion of the senses. Her body shook as tremors racked over her. His release joined hers. For a long moment, he stayed frozen above her, breath held.

Sebastjan rolled next to her, his arm touching hers. "I'm glad you came to me. I've been waiting for you every night."

"I think you put too much guilt on yourself for the wedding night," Ariella said. "The pain was really nothing to the bone pain I grew up with. I know people here like to treat me like I'm a delicate piece of silk, but I'm not."

"Mmm," Sebastjan moaned, reaching for her. He palmed a breast. "Are you sure? Your skin feels like silk."

She reached for his hand, touching it briefly before touching her shoulder. "It wasn't always. I used to have these scars everywhere. There was a long one across my shoulder. One of my sisters hit me with a ritual candlestick."

"I'm sorry you lost them."

"I was told it was quick." Even though she'd started the subject, she didn't want to talk about that. Not right now.

As if sensing her desire to change the topic, he said, "I know we are supposed to leave in a week, but I'd rather go sooner. I find it hard to breathe here. Would you mind?"

Ariella couldn't stop the grin from coming over her features. "I would really like that."

"If you don't mind my asking, why are you here? What happened to your family?"

Ariella stiffened, her smile fading. Perhaps he hadn't read her mind in that regard. "I told you. They were murdered on my plane. I was here, so I survived."

"We don't have murder," Sebastjan said. "What reason would someone have to do that?"

"There was a rebellion between the two ruling houses. My father represented the House of the Goddesses. The House of Gods attacked and killed him and my older sisters."

"Why?"

"It was discovered that my sisters were not pure. Vessels of the goddesses are meant to be pure. And the most ironic part of it all was that it was the sons of the gods who took their maidenhoods." She sighed, dropping her hand from where his fingers lightly rubbed her breast. "It all feels so far away. I was only supposed to be here for a few weeks. My bones were fragile. They broke all the time despite the precautions everyone took. That is how I got most of my scars. When Divinity Corporation came seeking to copy our sacred texts for inter-dimensional analysis and comparison, they offered to bring me here in return. I never saw my family again. Divinity brought pictures of the aftermath as well as a faithful servant to tell me the news. I couldn't go back. I don't know any other planes and had nothing to trade with Divinity to take me anyway."

"And we fixed you." Sebastjan drew his fingertip down her arm. He sounded so certain of the fact. They all did on this plane, as if they could cure everything—even death by old age. But the truth was, they had only managed to prolong life, not find the cure for the ultimate death.

"The Medical Supreme fixed my bones and took away my physical scars," she corrected. "He instituted my health regimen."

Suddenly, Sebastjan sat up on the bed. He turned to study her. For a long moment, he didn't say anything. Then, touching the side of her face, he asked, "Is that why you agreed to this? Gratitude?"

Gratitude? Ariella suppressed the urge to laugh, though she felt no humor in the idea. It wasn't gratitude. She hadn't even agreed. Not really. Still, as she looked at him, for all his newness to her, she couldn't help but think there could be more between them. He had a brooding quality to him. It shone in his eyes, as if he was trapped in the same cage she was in. Still, after less than a week, she didn't know him well enough to trust him.

Closing her eyes, she said the only truth she could, "I am grateful to no longer carry the sickness I had when coming here."

"IF YOU KNOW what is best for you, you will make him stay another week," Supreme Walter said without preamble as Ariella walked through the door.

"How do you propose I do that?" She stopped just inside the room, not approaching the desk.

"Tell him you wish to stay," Supreme Walter answered, as if it was the simplest thing in the world.

"But I don't," she said. Her warden raised a brow at her tone. "I never did."

"Such gratitude," he muttered.

"I'm really beginning to hate that word, gratitude. What should I feel gratitude for? My family being killed? Being held prisoner? Being on an alternate reality that is nothing like my real home? Saved only to be poisoned? Forced to marry? Forced to smile? Forced to...?" Ariella didn't know why, now, out of all the time she'd had these thoughts, that she allowed them to spill out of her mouth. She shrugged helplessly. "Sure. I'm grateful."

"I see my son is having an effect on you. I had rather hoped you would have had an effect on him." Supreme Walter stood. "Regardless. If you leave before the week is up, I won't give you the cure. If you tell my son, I won't give you the cure. I will have this my way. Do you really want to give up the rest of your life to deny me one week."

"One week? What's to stop you from—"

"If you don't stop talking and leave my office this instant, I won't give you the cure." His words were low, hard, and she saw the arrogance in every nuance of his expression.

"Don't make promises you don't intend to keep," she answered. So what if he didn't give her the cure. Sometimes she thought it might be better if he didn't.

"What was that?" he demanded.

"I said, I'll talk to him." Her words were faint as she backed away from the hateful man.

"See that you do."

SEBASTJAN FROWNED AT HIS WIFE, wondering at the sudden change in her demeanor. The night before, he'd felt as if they'd connected. They'd stayed up all night, talking, laughing, whispering, kissing. They even came together in the morning, finding sleepy release.

"You wish to stay?" Sebastjan sighed heavily. "I thought we discussed this."

"Your father insists," Ariella answered, as if that should have made a difference to him. "It is only for a week."

"Then it will be two weeks, then three. I know how the man works." Sebastjan frowned. "No. I'm leaving. We're leaving."

She refused to look at him, instead turning to stare at the hallway monitor. "I can't."

"Why?"

"I can't tell you."

"What does my father have on you?" Sebastjan reached for her face, but she pulled away from him.

"I can't tell you."

"What can you tell me?" He reached for her again, this time forcing her to meet his eyes.

Still she looked past his shoulder. "Nothing that pertains to this."

"You're my wife, but your loyalty belongs to

him." Sebastjan let her go. "I should have known there was more to this arrangement than what I was seeing." He sighed heavily, correcting himself, "I did know. I just didn't want to think about it."

"Sebastjan." The plea in her voice managed to stop him from walking away. "I want...I'm sorry I can't tell you."

When he looked in her eyes, something inside of him wanted to believe her, to trust her and help her. But all he really knew about her was that she came from tragedy to his home plane and married him because his father wanted it. "Fine. If you wish it, we will stay one more week. No more."

"One week. That is all," Sebastjan informed his father sternly. "Any more than that and I will be shirking my duties."

Ariella hated the pleased look on Walter's face as Sebastjan told him of their plans to stay. She took a quick bite of her food, hurrying to finish it so she could be excused.

Medical Supreme Walter didn't comment on his son's statement. "Have you finished your communications, Ariella?"

"Almost."

"Father," Sebastjan said, standing. "Excuse us."

Walter nodded. "Check your monitor. I've posted a schedule for this week for you."

Ariella pushed up from her seat and followed Sebastjan from the room. When they were alone, he said, "You looked like you wanted out of there as fast as I."

"I want out of this house," she admitted. "But if we go out the side door to the gardens he'll see the door alarm and will most likely join us."

"Not so. Come, I'll show you a way to escape undetected. I discovered it as a boy." He led the way to the side door and reached to the small computer next to the door. Touching the screen, he set the unit to do a detailed maintenance check. "If you enter my father's code, six-six-nine, the system will run a diagnostic that takes seventy three minutes. This door will remain undetectable for that time. It's a glitch in the security system. I know, because I programmed it in. Since my father doesn't trust anyone to touch the system, no one has ever bothered to fix it."

"You're not worried someone will break into this place?"

He pulled her with him outside. "Into the home of the Medical Supreme?" Sebastjan shook his head.

"Not likely. The only crime on this plane is stolen research and that is rare. Everything is documented."

Ariella felt the tension roll off her shoulders as the cool breeze caressed her skin. The glass walls holding in the trees surrounded the path, keeping the true smell of nature trapped. She breathed deeply. "I sometimes think about lighting a torch to melt through the glass walls, just so I can crawl in and lie on the grass."

"I wish I had a secret way into the gardens so I could take you." Sebastjan reached for her hand.

"You're not afraid of the pollen?"

"No. It was my grandfather who had an aversion to pollen. He boxed in all the plants. There are places, outside of Asclepius, where nature is not put away in boxes."

Ariella pulled him closer, drawing the hand clasped with his around her back so he was forced to hug her. "There are many things put away in boxes here."

"What do you mean?"

Ariella thought it best not to clarify. The night was beautiful, made even more so by the fact Walter didn't know where she was. It was the first time since she'd met the man that he didn't know her exact location. A giddiness filled her at the tiny taste of freedom. She looked up into Sebastjan's eyes, noticing how well his body fit against hers. Letting go of his hand, she ran her fingers up his arm. He didn't let go as he held her to his chest.

The stir of arousal filled her and was echoed back in the lift of his erection and soft sigh of his breath. She trembled in anticipation, wondering if he'd take her here on the garden pathway. Licking her lips, Ariella offered her mouth to him. He didn't deny her. His kiss was gentle, brushing over her lips until they parted to allow him deeper access.

Breaking free, he grabbed her hand and led her through the garden until the mansion became a blurred obscurity behind glass. Sebastjan pressed her against the glass wall. He cupped her cheek, turning her mouth back to his as he resumed the kiss. Soft noises escaped her and she moaned into him. His hands skimmed over her shirt, running down to lift her longer tunic.

She turned her face to take a deep breath. Sebastjan kissed her throat, biting along the flesh from her jaw to her ear. The combination of hard and soft caresses caused her to shiver. Ariella ran her hands over his chest, liking the feel of him. Her fingers found the hard curves and valleys of his muscles, liking the way he flexed against her touch.

When his hand found the flesh of her hip, baring her legs by pushing down her pants, she closed her eyes. She tugged at his waistband, pulling his pants to free his arousal. Her senses became sharp. Their light pants mingled, backdropped by the sound of wind against the plant boxes. The texture of his palm sweeping along her thigh contrasted the hard glass against her back.

Sebastjan lifted her leg. Ariella pulled at their tunics, trying push the disheveled clothing out of the way. He brought his hips to hers and she jerked with sensation at the intimate contact. Holding onto his neck, she let him pull her other leg up so she straddled his waist. He kept his hands on her ass as he drew his body to hers. He entered her slow and deep. Ariella wanted more. She hooked her ankles behind him, pulling him forward in harder thrusts.

Moonlight caressed his skin, shadowing and lighting his face. The blue tones changed the shade of his flesh, tinting it so it looked almost pale. She held on tighter, feeling free from the bonds of her imprisonment. The end felt so near—the end of threats and disease, the end of the tension building in her stomach. Hope welled inside her. Soon she'd be truly free, away from this awful city with its locks and bars. Perhaps this was why the goddesses sent her here. They were rewarding her for her pious life. They knew the House of Goddesses would be attacked and they saved her. They sent her to not only be cured, but to find Sebastjan.

All these thoughts swirled in her head, flowing through her consciousness like a sudden burst of understanding. In this moment, this perfectly blissful moment, it all made sense. The universe lined up and she understood. She didn't like all elements of the journey, but she felt the symmetry of it. The pleasure pushed her body over the edge. Her muscles tensed. Her nerves tingled. Her entire body jerked in helpless release.

Sebastjan thrust harder, his body pressing tight. He bit at her earlobe. "I want to devour you. I want this to last. I want to take you from here and—" The words were cut off as he came, trembling against her. He gripped her ass tight, as if to keep from dropping her.

Somewhere in the back of her mind, she longed to hear him finish the sentence. Another part of her was frightened of what he would say. He dropped her legs and their bodies pulled apart. Ariella reached to right her clothing and Sebastjan did the same.

"I don't want to go back inside," Sebastjan said,

but they both knew that they had to. There was a tenderness in him when he looked at her. Or perhaps she imagined it. The moonlight and passion could have been giving her more hope than was realistically plausible. "Come stay in my room with me tonight. I would have you sleep near."

Ariella nodded and they both silently walked back into her prison.

Days passed, yet Sebastjan found he didn't hate being at the mansion. Sure, he didn't care to be around his father, but the fact that every second of it was spent next to his new wife made up for the Medical Supreme's presence. Unfortunately, direct conversation with her was limited to stolen seconds between streams of social insipidness. And, for all her protesting to stay, Ariella seemed to enjoy it as little as he. Their only reprieve was the night, when nothing mattered beyond the boundaries of his bed.

He closed his eyes, wishing more than anything to be back there—hands roaming her flesh, lips exploring, bodies joining. Last night, they'd barely made it to his room. Her thigh had brushed his during the evening sustenance and he'd been lost in erotic thoughts of what he would do to her once he had her alone. He'd thrown her over the side of the bed, long shirt tossed up along her back and had his way with her. It had been wickedly wonderful.

"Are you ready?" Sebastjan asked, as Ariella's door slid open. He adjusted his hips, trying to hide the all-too-obvious evidence of his arousal. His breath caught as she turned. Her green eyes practically glowed because of the perfect green shade of her long shirt. The charcoal gray pants matched his shirt, an effect undoubtedly planned by his father's maid when she laid out their clothing the night before.

Ariella smiled, reaching to brush her long hair over her shoulders. She seemed completely unaware of the effect she had on him. "What is it we're doing again?"

"Greeting off-plane doctors," he answered. Sebastjan frowned. Dr. Gerard Fauchet would be there and he couldn't soon forget the man's flirting.

"Ah." She reached for his arm, trying to walk him from the room. "That sounds fascinating. What kind of plane are they from? Do they look like us? I've heard that on some planes the people can't be in the sunlight or they explode into ash. When I was on the Divinity base before coming here, some of the scientists were talking about the different worlds. Did you know that there are people with purple flesh? And a whole plane of people without a single hair on their body?" She looked excited by the prospect. "What if they have extra limbs, or—"

He chuckled, unable to help himself as he said, "Wait. Don't go yet." He pulled her back against his chest. The door lifted halfway and then drew back down as she came out of reach of the sensors.

"What...?" she began, only to stop when she felt the obvious press of his erection to her ass. "Oh. Now? Here?"

"Why not now?" He kissed the back of her ear. "Why not here?"

"We'll be late," she protested feebly. Ariella didn't try too hard to escape his caresses.

"So we'll be late. What can the Medical Supreme do to us? Look stern? Scold us again for not attending to our duties? Let him wait." This time he licked her ear. She shivered, melting into him. "Besides, I cannot greet off-plane doctors in my current state. Imagine the stories that will be told about this plane. They will think us all barbarians on Chiron who think of nothing but sex."

"Is it so far from the truth?" she teased. "Perhaps they would be flattered to be greeted with such inter-est. I've heard of alternate realities where the people walk about naked and have never heard of clothing. I would have to think they don't have snow where they live. Oh, and there are others who sell sexual favors like food on the street corners and no one thinks it strange. Still other planes are said to have men who are kept inside large, stone homes to be used for the whims of their women."

"Mm, are you saying you'd like to lock me inside a stone house and use me for your whims?" He grinned, part of him liking the idea, however unrealistic.

As if coming to a decision, she glanced at the closed door. "All right, you win, quick, out of those pants. We will have time if we hurry." She pulled up her shirt and began tugging at her waistband.

Sebastjan laughed, not needing to be told twice. He barely had them loosened around his hips when she pushed him toward a chair. The hard surface pressed into his naked ass. A narrow back supported him as he leaned into it, but there were no sides or arms.

Ariella kicked her pants aside and moved to straddle him. Her pussy was wet as she drew it along his shaft, attesting to how desperately she wanted him. She reached between them, enthusiastically angling his body to hers. With a light groan, she sat on his lap, impaling her body.

"Oh," she sighed, lifting up only to fall down. She gripped his shoulders, holding tight as she rode him. He took her by the hips and braced his feet on the floor, balancing their bodies as he let her have her way. "Perhaps this plane could be all about being sex-crazed barbarians. I love the way this feels."

She let her head fall back as she looked toward the ceiling. Her hips moved in hard, fast, desperate thrusts. Sexually engaging sighs left her in soft pants of air. Ariella jerked as she came, pressing down on him. The sight of her pleasure was too much. His release joined hers. Without giving them much time to bask in the aftermath, she stood and began to straighten her clothing. Sebastjan was much slower to follow.

When she finished redressing, she looked at him. Her cheeks were flushed and her eyes appeared to glisten with mischief. "Hurry. I'll meet you by the transport."

If he wasn't so sated he might have been hurt by her quick departure. Instead he grinned. The faster they did their duty the faster they could be done with it.

1 3

THE BOX-SHAPED VEHICLE moved soundlessly over the streets, hovering over the ground as it sped along Asclepius' self-navigating streets. Two rows of seats faced inward, making for easy conversation. Once the address was typed into the transport's computer, the occupants were free to enjoy the ride—no driver needed.

Ariella was not enjoying the ride. Medical Supreme Walter stared at her for most of it, clearly disappointed in her tardiness. She tried to ignore the sick feeling she got from the man's unwanted attention, endeavoring to focus her thoughts on Sebastjan. How the two could be related was beyond her understanding. But, the sameness in their physical appearance confirmed that they were indeed father and son.

"I expected lateness from my son," Walter had said when Ariella hurried down the stairs to join him, "but not from you. I expect better from you."

She reached for the buttons next to the window, pushing one so that the outside became more visible. They were slowing near the middle of town in front of the Central Hospital and Optimal Health Centre building. She recognized the giant structure with its thick Corinthian columns and oversized stone arches. Inside, the metal corridors would look nothing like the fine architectural façade.

As the transport stopped, the doors opened automatically, sliding to the side. Supreme Walter stepped out first, then Sebastjan, who then helped her down. Stone stretched as far as she could see—statues, sidewalks, streets and buildings. Only a little bit of plant life was allowed in the city, and that was blocked by large glass panels.

"Are you all right?" Sebastjan asked, not letting go of her arm.

"Fine," she lied. In truth, Ariella always found it a little hard to breathe in the sterilized environment.

"Is it because this is where the Divinity portal is stored?" he insisted. "Are you thinking of home?"

"Come on," Supreme Walter ordered. "They're waiting on us."

Inside, the metallic gray corridors of the hospital looked like an endless maze, only the orange lettering on the walls gave directions. Unfortunately for Ariella, she wasn't able to understand them. The smell of the hospital's air filtering sterilizer wafted over her. A loud alarm blared overhead, buzzing annoyingly.

"They've arrived," Supreme Walter said, walking faster. "They will be in sterilization right now to check for other dimensional parasites and viruses. We must hurry."

"Why is he so eager to greet these guests?" Ariella asked. "Does he want something from them?"

"He likes the attention," Sebastjan answered with a smirk.

Supreme Walter stopped ahead of them, greeting Dr. Lu. The man wore the standard issue uniform for the facility, a long blue coat with red trim. Like everyone else at the hospital, he kept his hair cropped short.

"Welcome back, Sans Ariella," Dr. Lu said to her before addressing her husband in quiet conversation. He carried an orange electronic clipboard, which he referred to several times. Sebastjan glanced at Ariella with a slight frown, nodding his head. Then, Dr. Lu reached into his pocket and took out a syringe. Like everything else it was electronic. He pressed the tip to the clipboard, waited for a beep and then leaned forward to inject it into Sebastjan's neck.

"We received word from the Starian ambassador, Sans Lady Lilith," Dr. Lu said as Sebastjan Ariella inched closer so she could listen to the conversation. "It looks like you will be receiving the blue mineral water you requested as soon as the Medical Supreme signs off on a shipment of handheld units."

Supreme Walter actually chuckled, like a kid in possession of a secret weapon. Sebastjan's whole body tightened but he managed to nod in response. "Thank you for making the arrangements, Dr. Lu."

"Yes, thank you, Dr. Lu," the Medical Supreme added.

Ariella shared at look with Sebastjan, wondering what he was thinking as he frowned back at her. She unconsciously touched her hair, smoothing it down. He said nothing as he turned his attention away.

A few minutes later, Ariella found herself standing before two off-plane women. One, a Dr. Cecilia Markos whose serious nature seemed well in tune with the people of Chiron, looked at the flirty Dr. Gerard Fauchet as if he'd grown two heads and had begun snorting fire. She had her brunette locks pulled back from her face, a stern look that suited the disdain on her face.

Dr. Markos' assistant, Sans Linnea Nel, seemed more easygoing. Her shoulder-length black hair had a streak of dark purple down the side. It matched the strange shade of her purplish-gray eyes. She chuckled, hiding her smile in the stack of papers she carried. To Ariella's somewhat disappointment, the visiting women's flesh was of normal color and they didn't have any visible abnormalities. In fact, they were quite ordinary.

"May I present the esteemed Dr. Swift?" The Medical Supreme nodded to the hospital's director. "Director of Central Hospital."

Ariella turned her smile to the director, having met him at a few social outings, but he barely glanced in her direction. The director eyed the newly arrived assistant's hair for a long moment before greeting Dr. Markos. Ariella always got the impression the man found himself too important to talk to the non-medical.

"Come with me."

Ariella stifled a gasp of surprise when Sebastjan whispered into her ear. He pulled her slowly back, leading her away from the others. No one seemed to notice their withdrawal. Well, no one but Linnea who smirked in their direction but said nothing.

Once outside in the corridor, he quickened his pace. Ariella giggled. Her body heated with the idea of getting him alone. She'd heard about the insatiable, those people who couldn't get enough of their lover. She never thought she'd become one of them.

Sebastjan leaned next to a closed door and let the retinal scanner read his eyes. The door slid open and he pulled her in.

"Welcome, Dr. Walter," an animated voice said.

Ariella came up behind him, reached for his ass, squeezing the firm cheek. He took a deep breath. She let her hand slide around his hip. To her surprise, he pulled away from her touch.

"I need you to step into the medical booth for scanning," Sebastjan said. "This is important."

Ariella looked around the private exam room, finally registering where they were. She forced all expression out of her face and all emotion from her voice. "Why?"

"I don't wish to alarm you, but Dr. Lu mentioned he found some anomalies in your scans. They have the most up-to-date equipment here. He has given me permission to use this room to test—"

"No." Ariella shook her head. "This isn't necessary. I'm fine. There's no need to—"

"It's just a scan. There's no reason to be scared," he tried to assure her. "I'll be right here the whole time."

"I'm fine. I swear it." Ariella looked at the booth. "It's being taken care of."

"Ariella," he insisted, stepping to block the door. Worry filled his eyes. "I'm a doctor. You're my wife. Why won't you let me scan you? What are you hiding?"

She took a step for the medical booth. Her hands shook as she touched the side. "It's a small thing. It's being taken care of."

"I insist."

"I—" The lasers turned on before she even stepped inside the scanner. She closed her eyes briefly before doing as he asked. Ariella hoped he'd find whatever it was his father had done to her.

A loud blare sounded overhead. Ariella screamed in surprise at the suddenness of it. Her back hit the wall in alarm.

"Containment," the automated system announced, as a plastic wall slid down from the ceiling, trapping her on one side of the room. "Containment. Exam one. Terminal. Containment. Security level one. Containment."

Ariella stared at Sebastjan's stunned face. The automated message repeated. Sebastjan reached for an electronic clipboard without looking directly at it. Instead, his eyes focused on hers as if he could read the cause of the sudden trouble in her face. His hand hit the wall several times before he found the device. His lips moved, but she couldn't hear him. She shook her head in denial, motioning to her ears.

"Containment. Exam one. Terminal. Containment."

14

"SEBASTJAN! What is the meaning of this? What have you done?" Supreme Walter demanded from the exam room door. It had taken nearly fifteen minutes for it to open after Ariella's containment started. The facility sensors had been testing the exam room air to make sure it and Dr. Sebastjan Walter were safe. "We have equipment at home. You should never have brought her in here."

Sebastjan glared at his father. "Did you know about her condition? Why haven't the home monitors picked up on it?"

"Of course I know," his father quipped. "I know everything that happens in my city. You're first doctor on scene. Clear her so we can go home. I will deal with the two of you in private."

"Then you also know it's not a natural condition," Sebastjan insisted, ignoring the threat. He looked at Ariella, knowing she couldn't hear them. She stood against the plastic shield, hands lifted, palms and fingers pressed so hard they turned white. Her large eyes stared at them. She looked terrified.

"Of course I know." The Medical Supreme frowned. "Clear her. Now."

"What did you do? Program the home monitors so they wouldn't show her abnormality?" Sebastjan refused to hand over the clipboard. "What's wrong with her? Did you think to trick me into marrying someone who is...sick?"

Sebastjan's stomach tightened. He again looked at his clipboard. The anomaly didn't make sense. It wasn't natural, but he'd never seen anything like it. He began tapping the electronic interface, examining the molecular structure.

"It's not a—" Sebastjan began.

"It's nothing you'd recognize." His father snatched the clipboard away. "Perhaps if you had stayed here and worked with me like I'd asked you to."

"You mean like you ordered me to," Sebastjan corrected as he tried to grab the clipboard back. "What did you do to Ariella?"

"You should thank me. I trained her to be the perfect doctor's wife. She will do as she's told and if she doesn't..." Supreme Walter set the clipboard down decisively. "Clear her now or you can forget about my signing off on those handhelds and any future funding for your research facility."

"That threat is empty and we both know it. Besides, I've already authorized the posting of my preliminary findings to several predominate scientists. I'd like to see you explain your reasoning to them."

"Don't threaten me, son. You're not skilled enough for it."

"It wasn't a threat."

Sebastjan looked at his wife. She stared at his father. Her face was hard, but he saw the fear in her eyes. He tried not to believe his father capable of anything so diabolical. Sure, the man was manipulative and shrewd, but this? Would his father really go so far as to poison a woman just to control her?

"This is how you got her to marry me, isn't it? You made sure she was well and then forced her to marry me by holding the cure hostage from her." He felt sick to his stomach and his heart began to beat a little faster. The wall monitor instantly brought up his stats.

Supreme Walter eyed the wall unit and frowned. "Calm yourself. I did it for you, for the family. You refused to consider any of the women I found for you. Dr. Sanda had too much invested in the marine facility. Sans Franuk was too tall. Sans Gretchen too obnoxious and attention seeking. Sans Angeluv too messy. Ariella is perfect for you. I've made sure of it. The only way I could have found you a more malleable bride is if I built a woman from scratch. If it were possible, I would have done so. But I am merely a man."

Sebastjan frowned. The humble words hardly suited the Medical Supreme. He'd begun to feel something for Ariella, but now, with his father's words, he became worried. What if the woman he knew was merely an act orchestrated by his father? What if her behavior, her attraction toward him, was pretend? What if her affections ended with her illness?

"If you're not pleased with her lack of experience, train her or take a lover. You're married now. That's all I care about. Procedures can be done to ensure she has a legitimate son and the family name will be carried on." Supreme Walter walked to the isolation chamber and tapped on the clear plastic, like examining a specimen in a jar. Ariella pulled away from him, edging to the far side of the chamber. "Let her out of there. You see how scared she is. The longer this continues, the more you risk damaging our reputations."

"Reputations?" Sebastjan demanded, enraged. "You poison a woman and you're worried about how it will look for your reputation? Maybe you should have thought about that before you did what you did. You want her cleared? Fine. Tell me then, how do we reverse whatever it is you've done? Can you even reverse it?"

"Of course I can."

Sebastjan closed his eyes briefly before grabbing the clipboard. He began tapping instructions on the top of it.

"What are you doing?" the Medical Supreme demanded. "Give me that."

Sebastjan jerked away from him. "I'm sending a copy of her medical records to my facility office. If you don't cure her, I'll make what you've done public."

"You wouldn't dare."

Sebastjan cleared his wife, ending her isolation. The plastic shield slid up and a light, sterilizing mist sprinkled over them. Ariella was breathing heavy and shaking. Her eyes flew to Supreme Walter. "They must have scanned me when we walked in. I didn't know this would happen. I didn't say anything. I promise I didn't say anything."

"She's making a scene. Take her, Sebastjan, and meet me at home. I'll take care of Dr. Lu and Dr. Swift." Supreme Walter stormed from the room, mumbling under his breath.

"Come with me, Ariella. All will be well." Sebastjan took her arm and led her toward the door. "Let's get out of here. We can talk in the transport."

15

"I wanted to tell you," Ariella said the second the transport door closed and they were alone. "I never meant to keep it from you."

"You should have told me." Sebastjan's brow furrowed in concentration as he studied her from the opposite seat. She wondered what he was thinking. It was impossible to tell.

"He said if I told you he'd take away my cure and I'd die a horrific death." She looked at her hands, studying the lines. "I tried to get away once, to test it. Within six hours I was..." Her hands began to shake at the memory. It started with nausea and built into a blinding headache. She'd been stumbling and incoherent. When Supreme Walter found her, she'd been curled into a ball. He'd only given her relief after she begged for it.

"Tell me," Sebastjan urged crossing over to sit beside her.

Ariella obeyed and told him everything. What did she have to lose now? Besides, his nearness was comforting—his smell, the sound of his voice, the brush of his leg to hers, the gentle tug of his fingers against her hair. When she finished, she added, "I wanted to tell you, but I wasn't sure what he'd do. I'm still not sure. I've seen that look on his face before. He's not happy and he's capable of mean things when he's not happy."

"I see." Sebastjan loosened his hold on her. "That is his game. He thinks to keep you at his house and by extension keep me. I'm sorry you were brought into this. My father was not pleased when I left Asclepius. He wants to groom me to be Medical Supreme, to keep the title in the family."

"You don't want to be Medical Supreme?" Even as she said it, she knew his answer. No. She saw the light in his eyes when he talked about going back to his research facility. He wanted out of the mansion as badly as she did.

"No. I have no use for the politics that consume my father's life. I want to do research and make a real difference in the future of my people. That will be my legacy, not approving funding proposals and hosting evening sustenance parties."

"I think yours will be the nobler legacy." Ariella took a deep breath. Her words soft, she asked, "Do you think you can cure what he did?"

"Given enough time."

"Within six hours?" She gave a wry laugh, not finding humor in her situation.

Sebastjan looked as if he wanted to tell her yes, but he slowly shook his head in denial. "No, not in six hours, not even if I had a fully stocked lab at my disposal. In six months if I was lucky, six weeks if I was very lucky."

Ariella leaned toward the transport window and looked out over the passing city. Light gleamed on the cases surrounding the plants and glistened on the perfect sidewalks, reflecting like tiny jewels. As the mansion came into view, she said, "I don't want to go back to the mansion. Not yet."

Sebastjan reached for the consul, overriding the transport's automatic coordinates. "I'll set it to take us through the arboretum. It won't be too busy this time of day."

She swayed into him as the transport turned a corner. Ariella found comfort in the heat of his body close to hers and didn't pull back. His hand trailed down the side of her arm. "You should leave. Go back to your research facility. I'm not sure he'll ever give me a cure. Take samples of my blood, or whatever else you need with you. Maybe someday when you find what's wrong with me, you can come back. I can't leave and I can't ask you to stay here. There is no reason why we should both be held prisoner."

Sebastjan didn't answer right away. "I won't leave you with him. I promise. We'll find a way to make you well."

Ariella drew her mouth to his. When they touched, he felt so familiar, as if she'd known him her whole life. She trusted him on a base, primitive level, even if logic told her she hadn't known him long enough.

"There are some things you just know," she whispered against his lips, answering her own thought.

"What?" He pulled away, quizzical.

"Nothing," she quickly amended. She placed her hand on his strong thigh, feeling it flex. "I was merely thinking of the arboretum. You said it wasn't going to be busy this time of day?"

"It—" Sebastjan's breath caught as she slid her hand higher, "shouldn't, ah, be."

"Good." She boldly cupped her hand around his growing member and massaged gently. He opened his thighs as he adjusted his hips on the seat. He sat back, allowing her complete access to his body. She tugged at his clothing, wanting him naked. Ariella jerked the pants from his hips and pushed his shirt aside.

Sebastjan's hands were on her, stripping her of her clothing as she continued to stroke him to full arousal. The transport turned, rocking them to the left. A flash of green passed outside the window as they turned into the arboretum. Ariella loved this place. Though separated from their human visitors, the green landscape stretched before them—trees, flowers and shrubs. Workers in stark white containment suits moved through the gardens, tending the foliage, picking up fallen leaves, plucking dying flowers.

When they were naked, Sebastjan pulled her body over his. She straddled his legs, balancing on the seat. He held on to her, keeping her from falling back. Hungrily, he pulled a nipple deep into his mouth. Moaning, he sucked and licked.

She tried to angle her body to accept his, but he held tight to her hips, gripping her hard. His lips moved to the opposite side, wetting the nipple he found there. Ariella tried again to impale her pussy on his shaft. He gently pushed her back.

"Sit," he urged, pushing her across the transport to the opposite seat.

Her ass pressed against the smooth, comfortable surface. Sebastjan's eyes lit as knelt before her on the transport floor. He nudged the inside of her knee, lifting her calf onto his shoulder. He kissed along the inside of her thigh, making the torturously slow journey up her leg. Lips pressed, tickled, brushed and sucked. His tongue flicked along her flesh, marking his path with delicate sweeps. Ariella tensed as he made his way toward the apex of her thighs. A firm hand on her thigh pressed it open.

"You look very beautiful in daylight," Sebastjan said, jerking her hips forward. He wrapped his arm under her leg, keeping it on his shoulder, as he kept the other one held open. He licked his lips slowly. His eyes flickered with meaning. "I want to watch you find release."

He buried his face in her pussy. Ariella gasped, arching into him. Her eyes lazily moved to the window, watching for anyone who might be looking inside.

Sebastjan moaned, fucking her with his mouth. He nipped at her clit, biting lightly before sucking it between his teeth. She grabbed onto the back of his head, rocking into him. His tongue slid along her sex, dipping inside her before moving up the slit.

Ariella gasped, grabbing her breasts as pleasure rippled over her. It was wicked and wanton and they could be caught at any moment should the transport pass anyone walking along the arboretum path. The hint of danger heightened her excitement. Her heart beat faster. She worked her legs against Sebastjan. He didn't stop, even as his eyes lifted to watch her.

It felt so good that she had to close her eyes. Tremors racked over her, radiating from her pussy, over her stomach and thighs. She came against his mouth, gasping and jerking.

When his lips finally stopped moving and he withdrew from her, she looked at him. He took a seat across from her. She breathed hard. He sat naked. His hand brushed along his leg, slow and steady.

Taking his cock in hand, he stroked himself. His eyes roamed freely over her naked body. He licked his wet lips, moaning softly as if he could still taste her on them. His hand tightened, sliding up and down his thick shaft.

Ariella's body began to tingle with anticipation. His lips had been nice, but she wanted the fullness of him moving inside her, thrusting and filling, pushing and pulling. The needy ache filled her and she touched her sex. Her fingers slid in the moisture left from his mouth.

She glanced around the inside of the transport, wondering how best to position herself so they could come together. As if reading her mind, he said, "Get on your knees and face the window."

Ariella turned to the side, drawing her knees onto the cushioned seat. He came behind her, forcing her to crawl closer to the window so he could fit. Sebastjan braced one foot on the floor and one knee on the seat. He took her by her hips.

The tip of his cock probed her sex as he positioned their bodies. With a groan, he impaled her on his shaft. Ariella saw his passing reflection in the windowpane as a ray of light broke through the trees.

He took her hard and sure, somehow managing to keep their bodies together in the precarious position. Her hands dug into the cushion. They slammed together wildly. Tremors worked over her as she came again. His cry joined hers as he met with release.

Sebastjan fell back. She collapsed next to him, nestling against his chest. He kissed her temple and wrapped his arms around her. For a long moment, they didn't speak. The plant life passed in silence.

"Are you certain every place on this plane doesn't keep its plant life encased?" Ariella asked, more whimsical than searching for an answer she already knew. "I miss the smell of nature. I think I'm going to scream if I'm misted with sterilizer one more time."

"Have you never been out of the city?" he asked, before answering his own question. "Of course you haven't. My father doesn't like to travel out of the city. He thinks everyone outside of high social circles of Asclepius are unworthy of his time."

"Let's not talk about him," she said. An unspoken tension fell over them. They had no choice but to go back to the mansion and face Supreme Walter.

"Agreed." Sebastjan pulled her closer. "Only the larger cities keep their nature locked up thanks to the old Medical Supreme's edict. Where I live we're much more relaxed. We even have a courtyard filled with flowers and vines."

"I wish I could show you my home world. It's nothing like this. Asclepius is so sterile, not only literally, but in its art. Everything is carved in straight lines. We have these beautiful sculptures—bold rounded figures, fanciful expressions, as if the human figure was captured in all its perfections and imperfections before being put into stone."

His hand moved lazily over her breast. "Perhaps someday we'll go there."

"Perhaps." Though Ariella knew she would never go back. Without her family, her home would be a hollow shell of what she remembered. At least this way, her family lived in her memory and she could imagine they were still out there, surviving on a plane of reality she couldn't see. Maybe even now, they stood, outside the transport box, as invisible to this world as air, running and laughing just beyond her range of vision.

"We should get dressed. The scenic trail will end soon and the transport will take us back." He kissed her temple. "I think I have an idea how to deal with my father."

"What will you do?"

"What he's been trying to get me to do for a long time now. I'm going to act like he does."

16

"You'll be happy to know that your indiscretion today will not be on record," Supreme Walter said as Ariella and Sebastjan joined him for their evening sustenance.

Sebastjan glanced at his wife, remembering all too well what they'd done in the transport. He hadn't meant for it to happen, but when Ariella looked at him he couldn't resist her. She hesitated, her hand gripping the back of her chair.

"Our indiscretion?" Ariella asked when no one spoke. She moved slowly to take a seat.

"I spoke with Dr. Lu and Dr. Swift," Supreme Walter continued, taking a small taste off the plate in front of him. Sebastjan hid his sigh of relief when he realized his father meant the quarantine. He didn't want to talk about his private moments with Ariella. "They will be enjoying their new equipment acquisitions purchased from your laboratory's budget."

"I want you to cure whatever it is you did to Ariella," Sebastjan stated as he took his seat at the long, metal table.

"I will not be dictated to," Supreme Walter stated. He took another bite. Sebastjan knew it was an effort to look calm and controlled. Inside, the man would be raging mad.

"I want you to cure whatever it is you did to Ariella," Sebastjan repeated, keeping his tone even, "or it won't just be my lab's budget that ends up paying people off. I'll take her to every facility in the city and have her scanned. Then, just for fun, I'll spread the rumor that every public building needs to upgrade for viruses because there's something new and nasty that slipped through the Divinity portals. I'll whisper and hint and others will listen because I am your son. Your reign as Medical Supreme will be known as a time of disease and chaos."

"You are bluffing. You wouldn't dare cause a planetary panic just to get even with me." Supreme Walter smiled. "You take your position as a doctor too seriously. Panic and chaos lead to injury and death."

"What I want you to ask yourself," Sebastjan pushed up from the table without touching his food, "is whether my sense of duty as a doctor outweighs my dislike of you and everything you stand for."

His father's smile instantly faded.

"Ariella?" Sebastjan motioned for her to follow him. She stood, not speaking. To his father, he said, "You have three hours to arrange it. We'll be waiting for your answer. Oh, and while we're discussing it, leave my laboratory's budget alone."

17

"I CAN'T BELIEVE you said all those things to him. When you said you were going to act like him, I thought you meant you were going to do something asinine or worse, like try to take his job as Medical Supreme." Ariella could barely contain her excitement, even as Sebastjan seemed stiff and irritated from dealing with Supreme Walter. "Did you see his face? He was speechless. I've never seen him speechless. His mouth actually opened and he didn't know what to say."

Sebastjan chuckled at her words. He relaxed some as he led her up the mansion stairs toward her room.

"I love you for that," she continued. Then, realizing what she'd said, she stopped walking. "I mean, I love...that...you did that."

His eyes softened. "I knew what you meant."

"I mean, I appreciate what you said to him." Ariella swallowed nervously as he looked at her. Why was she still justifying her statement? The monitor on the wall beeped, capturing her attention. She blushed to see that her heartbeat was elevated and that several of her levels had risen. The screen informed that a shot had been ordered to calm her. When she glanced at Sebastjan's stats, she saw that he also had elevated levels.

"Would you like to find out?" He cupped her cheek, tracing her lips with his thumb.

"Find out?" She looked at him, curious.

"It's a series of chemicals the body produces. We traded medical research with another plane that had done extensive mapping of brain chemicals. They're easy enough to read."

"What is?"

"They call the chemical phenylethylamine—"

"No," Ariella stopped him. "Not what it's called. I won't understand what you're saying anyway. Find out what? What is a series of chemicals?"

"Emotions." His fingers slid along her throat,

gently pressing into her hair only to pull out again. "Happiness. Love."

"Oh, I think that someone would know, I mean, the test isn't necessary for the..." She had no clue what she was saying. "Does it matter to you how I feel?"

The question seemed to surprise him. "Of course it matters. You're my wife. I know we didn't meet as couples normally do, but we both chose each other despite the persuasion of my father. There is an easiness between us, even a friendship. I care what you think and how you feel."

Ariella hadn't expected such candor from him. She'd seen his kindness, felt it in his touch, but she'd never expected him to express it in words. She wasn't sure she could be as articulate at the moment. She glanced at the monitor, feeling exposed by the way it told anyone who looked of her fast heartbeat, her quickened breath. But more poignantly, she felt exposed by the fact that he could read what the monitors said better than she could. "I care for you as well."

"I think that is a good start." Sebastjan drew her forward and pressed his mouth to hers. His tongue slid past her lips, hungrily devouring her with his passion. She stiffened for the briefest of moments before melting against him. All thoughts filtered out of her mind until all she could feel was the man before her.

She backed him toward the wall. His head bumped the monitor and he groaned. When she would have pulled back, he kept her from leaving him. He slid along the wall to a more comfortable position.

His hands moved freely over her clothes, fumbling to unbutton her shirt. His hand slipped beneath the material, enveloping her breast in his palm. He pinched her nipple. The sensitive bud peaked at the attention.

Ariella pulled at his clothing, reaching to the front of his pants. She rubbed his arousal, moaning softly to find him ready for her.

Suddenly, he pushed her back. "Ariella, wait."

She blinked, shocked that he stopped her until she saw him looking down the stairwell.

"We should go..." He looked toward his room.

"Come on," Ariella pulled him with her, moving to her room instead. It was closer and she wasn't sure she could wait. She needed him, wanted him. Her skin begged for his touch. Her nerves tingled with anticipation. The door slid open and she hurried through.

"Sans Ariella, I have your—ah!"

Ariella pulled away from Sebastjan at the sound of the maid's shock. She glanced around her husband, quickly adjusting her clothing.

"I have your injection." The maid lifted a shot.

Sebastjan growled under his breath, reaching for the shot. "I'll give it to her. Go."

The maid rushed from the room and the door shut behind her.

Ariella chuckled. She automatically leaned her head to the side. Sebastjan tossed the shot onto the floor, not bothering to inject her.

"But..." Ariella made a move to go after it.

"Leave it," he said. "No more medicine from my father's house. No more food. No more anything."

"No more anything?" Ariella pouted her lower lip. She reached forward to cup his cock. "Anything?"

Sebastjan chuckled. Instead of answering, he tore off his shirt and threw it over the syringe. Ariella tugged at her clothes, eagerly stripping. When they came together, naked flesh pressed against flesh. She reached between them and stroked his arousal. His breathing deepened, catching in his throat.

"I want you," she whispered, nipping at his ear.

Sebastjan spun her around, placing her on the

bed. The swift action pulled her hand from his arousal. He ground his hips into her, undulating as she rocked up to join him. His cock rubbed along the wet folds of her pussy, stroking just right. Cream moistened her sex, allowing him to glide against her.

"I want you, too," he said, the word a hoarse growl of emotion as he drew the tip of his shaft to enter her.

Sebastjan pushed up. He grabbed her by the back of her knee, pulling it up to better allow for his claiming. Then, with a hard push, he plunged into her depths, burying himself to the hilt. Her pussy tightened around him.

Ariella met his thrusts with her own. Their hips slammed together. And even though they were bound by the prison walls of her room, she felt free because she had hope. The sensations of ecstasy built.

She came, stiffening beneath him. Sebastjan answered her body's call, releasing into her. He collapsed next to her. His tousled hair and flushed features were more handsome than anything she'd ever seen.

A slow smile curled the side of his mouth. "Pack your things. We're leaving here the second you're cured."

18

ARIELLA PEERED at the Medical Supreme across the Central Hospital meeting room. She wished she could hear what the doctors were saying. According to Supreme Walter, she'd be cured within the hour—just as soon as he finished a procedure. Dr. Lu stood next to him, looking stern and slightly irritated. Next to them, Sebastjan crossed his arms as he listened to everything his father said. Since she wasn't a doctor with medical clearance, Ariella had not been allowed into the conversation.

When Sebastjan glanced at her, he gave her a small, comforting smile. She returned the look, lifting her hand in acknowledgement. It seemed like an eternity before they motioned her to come over. She did, crossing the distance until she stood across from Sebastjan.

"You have to take a trip through the portal. Arrangements have been made with a plane we have trade agreements with," Sebastjan said.

"I'm being traded?" Ariella gasped.

"No, don't be ridiculous," the Medical Supreme said. "Dr. Lu, leave us." Dr. Lu nodded his head and stepped out of the room. "I designed what you have to dissipate if you were to use Divinity's portal. It's the only way to get rid of what you have."

Ariella stiffened. The way the man said it, so matter-of-fact, so unapologetic. She frowned. "So no one would know what you did if I managed to run away to a plane you don't control."

"I liked you better before I married you to my son," Supreme Walter stated.

"But she's right, isn't she?" Sebastjan frowned. "If she's going, then I'm going though the portal too."

"You can't," Ariella denied. "I don't trust him." She turned to the Medical Supreme. "I don't trust you."

"Like I would abandon my only son on a primitive plane with a bunch of barbarians." Supreme Walter eyed her as if she were a stupid girl.

I really hate you, she thought, but kept quiet.

"Dr. Lu knows we are going. The blue mineral water is too important to this plane to risk ruining a trade agreement with Staria. If we don't come back, Staria will be blamed and our people will demand we take action." Sebastjan took Ariella by the arm. "We're ready. We'll go, make the trade, and be back."

"I'll have them dial the gate," Supreme Walter said.

"No, I'll get the coordinates from Dr. Lu. I'll dial it myself." Sebastjan led Ariella from the meeting room.

Ariella watched as Sebastjan turned dials and pressed buttons on the inter-dimensional portal's consul. Behind them, the square arch of the Divinity portal looked innocuous, like some badly chosen piece of decoration thrust against the wall. A blue glow filled the room, directed at the arch. The arch hid a complex configuration of liquid crystals, electrical currents, mirrors and vacuums. When activated, it was held in check by the wavelength of a specific blue light, which kept the portal inactive. Should the light change, a dimensional shift would occur taking whoever stood on the platform to a new parallel universe.

"Are you nervous? You said you've never dimension traveled before." Ariella stroked his arm.

"No. I am fine," he said. Twelve turn dials indicated the color coding, including intensity and saturation.

"I remember the stories people used to tell of the portals. I was so scared the first time I stepped through. Apparently, in the early days, before they made these destination platforms, travel was a haphazard affair and many of the testers died by materializing inside solid objects. Now Divinity sends out microscopic probes to new planes first."

When all the dials were all set, the blue shifted into a brilliant red light. Sebastjan grinned. "Maybe a little nervous. I'm happy you will be cured and excited to see what another world looks like."

"What do you think your father would do if we never come back?" Ariella asked, chuckling. "Have you ever thought about it? Just going to a new dimension and never coming back here?"

Sebastjan didn't answer. He took her hand and walked toward the platform. The closer they got, the more the light lured them in. Suddenly, the strong gravitational field pulled her off her feet, tearing her hand from his and hurling her toward the back of the platform.

Ariella, knowing what was to come, tucked her arms in and closed her eyes tight. The concentrated red light burned her flesh and every cell in her body felt as if it had turned to lead. She couldn't move, even as her body was pulled apart on a molecular level. Seconds later, the sensations stopped and her body was dropped onto a hard surface with a heavy thud.

Coughing, she automatically rolled to the side. Sebastjan nearly landed on top of her. All around them, the blue glow shone. Ariella searched her surroundings. They were in a cavelike clearing. The stone walls were etched with the tool marks made to carve them. A domed arch with a back and two side walls covered the platform. Every Divinity portal had a different look to it, but the main construct remained the same.

Sebastjan pushed up. "Ariella? How are you? How do you feel?"

Ariella gave a weak laugh and moaned, "Ow. I hate that part."

"I didn't imagine portal travel would be so painful." He took a deep breath and felt along his limbs as if checking to be sure they were still intact.

"It gets more bearable with time," came a woman's voice, "or perhaps we just get used to it."

Sebastjan helped Ariella to her feet.

"Welcome to Battlewar Castle. I'm Lady Lilith of Firewall. I will be your contact while you are here." Lady Lilith smiled. Her straight blonde hair fell freely about her shoulders and she had kind blue eyes. The tight fit of her white corset outlined her waist and hips, showcasing a generous amount of cleavage. Long skirts billowed around her legs, the dark crimson a stark contrast to the white. Ariella tried not to stare. "You must be new to portal travel. Though, if I recall correctly from my visits to plane 187, not many of your people have stepped through the portal. You usually have people brought to you. I am honored you would come."

Behind the woman, a bodyguard stood, his arms crossed in a protective gesture. He was a burly figure, dressed in a hard leather jerkin and dark breeches. Metal diamonds plated the leather, creating a symmetrical pattern over his thick chest.

"I am Dr. Sebastjan Walter and this is my wife, Ariella," Sebastjan said. "We are honored you would have us for your guests."

"Married?" Lilith looked Ariella over. "That's

probably for the best. Single women tend to get claimed rather quickly around here."

"Yes, I'm married," Ariella confirmed, inching closer to her husband.

"Walter, you say?" Lilith arched a brow. "As in Medical Supreme Walter?"

"The same," Sebastjan acknowledged. "He is my father."

"Will there be more of you?" Lilith glanced at the platform. "The Medical Supreme usually travels with at least a dozen armed men when he leaves your capital city—or so I've been informed."

Sebastjan led Ariella forward into the cave. Her legs shook nervously. All she had seen was a cave, a woman and one guard and she could still tell this world was going to be unlike any she'd ever dreamed of seeing. Sebastjan said, "No. We come alone. No guards. Your intentions in negotiation have never been hostile. When we knew you as Divinity Analyst Sans Lilith Grian, you always treated us fairly. I'm sure we'll be able to negotiate for the supplies you need."

Though hardly tense, Lilith seemed to relax at his words. She motioned toward a stairwell. "Please, follow me."

They walked through mazelike corridors of blue-gray stone. Torches burned from their places on the wall. Ariella breathed deeply, loving the smell of stone and fire. The ever so subtle hint of dust tickled her nose.

Lady Lilith brought them to a large dining area. Bright light came from a large fireplace along a far side of the room. Woven tapestries lined the walls in strips of material, showcasing coats of arms and various symbols.

A few warrior men sat at the tables, whispering amongst themselves. Though gruff in appearance, most of them looked recently bathed. Some wore lightweight tunics, others leather jerkins like the guards, others light chainmail and pieces of armor, and still others wore no shirt at all. Big metal goblets had been set before them, next to matching pitchers. She'd thought the guards were scary, but some of these men were practically gigantic. Muscles bulged, littered with puckered scars and tattooed designs.

When Lilith saw Ariella looking around, she said, "Battlewar Castle may look rough, but that is to be expected from a fortress designed by men constantly at war. Hopefully though, that will change now that this plane has found some peace. That is why there aren't too many warriors here now. They've all gone home to their families. As you can see, this plane is fairly rustic when compared to 187, but I assure you, you have nothing to fear."

"Oh, I'm not frightened. It reminds me of home in some ways. More so than 187." Ariella took another deep breath. "Smells like it too."

"You are not from 187?" Lilith asked.

"No, but it's my home now." Ariella refused to say more and Lilith didn't ask. Sebastjan's hand slid across her back in reassurance.

"Please join me at the high table. We can go over the details and, considering everything goes well, there will be a celebration tonight in honor of a successful negotiation." Lilith smiled. "We at Staria love any reason to celebrate."

19

"How are you feeling? It's been six hours," Sebastjan touched his wife's arm. He knew he was concerned without reason. She smiled brightly at him, her cheeks flushed, her laugh warm, her eyes bright.

Turning her gaze from where she looked over the hall of Starian people, Ariella leaned over to kiss him. "I'm well. I promise. Now, try your drink. You wouldn't want to be rude."

Sebastjan looked at the goblet before him. He liked to think he was open-minded and didn't live in fear, but having been raised on a sterile planet, with sustenance that was specifically designed for him, he found himself apprehensive to try what the Starians put before them.

At Ariella's playfully challenging gaze, he lifted the goblet to his lips and sipped. The sweet flavor was strange, like nothing he'd ever had before, and though completely different he couldn't help sipping again.

"You look like a child who was just given his first sweet." Ariella laughed.

Sebastjan took another drink. The hall erupted into a crescendo of good-natured laughter and cheering, though he hardly thought the merriment directed at his bravery in tasting the foreign drink. The men who filled the large area were boisterous and loud and covered in primitive black markings and scars. The women danced and laughed and teased. He'd never seen any gathering of people so happy. A raw, potent energy radiated from them—expressed in male posturing, female temptations and an unapologetically open sexuality.

"Mm," Ariella whispered against his ear. "I'm proud of you. That couldn't have been easy for you to try a drink from here."

As the heat from her lips brushed against him, Sebastjan took a deep breath. Lust threaded through his veins, emanating from the drink in his stomach, filtering through his limbs, filling his cock. A few of the couples in the crowd kissed passionately and, though he couldn't be one hundred percent sure, he thought he'd seen a couple of women slip beneath the tables to pleasure their men.

"I see you're not like your father in many ways," Lilith said, joining them. Her cheeks were flushed and her eyes glistened with an inner mischief. Sebastjan stiffened, glad the table hid his arousal. "He never partakes of our foods."

A giant of a man sat next to Lilith. He snorted at her comment but didn't speak. Dark hair framed his face in thick waves, not so long as to touch his shoulders. His eyes were a hard brown, until he looked at Lilith. Then they softened.

Sebastjan relaxed and smiled. Feeling strangely calm, he said, "My father and I agree on very little."

Lady Lilith knew a lot about his homeworld, having been there several times before her present assignment on Staria. The few times he'd met with her, he found her likable and easy to talk to. She had been a great source of information about this new plane and was the whole reason trade had been set up between Staria and Chiron in the first place.

"May I present my husband, Lord Sorin of Firewall," Lilith said, gesturing to the big man next to her.

"Welcome," Sorin said, nodding. Like the other

men, his manners and voice were gruff. He exuded an almost violent charm, as if at any moment he'd jump up from his seat and begin to fight. Looking at the man's fists, Sebastjan knew he'd be deadly.

"I've ordered rooms readied for you, should you decide to stay," Lilith said, leaning forward to look at Ariella. "You are most welcome. I'd be happy to show you around the city market tomorrow. You might enjoy it."

"Can we?" Ariella asked him. Sebastjan saw her excitement and nodded. Her hand brushed his leg. At that moment, he'd give her almost anything.

Have you ever thought about it? Just going to a new dimension and never coming back here? Her words echoed through him. In that moment, if she were to ask him to leave everything behind for her, he'd say yes.

"Wonderful!" Lilith announced. She continued to speak, but Sebastjan couldn't think past the hand resting on his thigh.

Ariella grinned, knowing she had to look like a drunken fool but unable to help it. The heady liquor affected her body. Even the meal of warm bread, seasoned meats and delicious cheeses couldn't counteract the effects of the alcohol. She wasn't sure she wanted it to. Staria wasn't exactly home, but it was strong and primal and the exact opposite of Chiron.

Somewhere in the hall a woman screamed playfully. The sound was followed by a sharp rise in male laughter. Lilith paused in her conversation with her husband. It was clear to all she was in love with the man.

Ariella turned her gaze to Sebastjan. "I like being here. It's almost like my visit to Asclepius never happened."

"I'm glad it did," Sebastjan answered. His eyes had a slight glaze to them. Fingers slid onto her thigh, massaging the muscle. "If you never visited my world, we wouldn't be here now." His hand moved to her hip. "We never would have met." He touched her waist, drawing her against his side. "I think to never have met you would have been a sad thing indeed."

Sebastjan turned to Lilith, whispering to the woman. Within moments, a guard was leading them through the passageways toward a private sleeping chamber complete with trunk, large fur-covered bed and a disturbing amount of weaponry hanging on the wall. A fire burned in a fireplace, heating the room and casting it with flickering orange light.

"This place." Sebastjan looked around. "It's like a child's tale from school. I feel like I've stepped into a book."

"I felt like that the first time I went through the portals," Ariella admitted. She pulled on his shirt, drawing him near. "I walked around, feeling as if nothing was real or that I'd stepped into some sort of strange underground society on my world instead being in a Divinity facility."

"Oh, I definitely feel as if this world is real." He grinned, stroking her cheek. "Very real, and soft, and pretty and—"

Ariella laughed, cutting him off. "And perhaps a little drunk?"

"Perhaps a little. I've never felt quite like this from the liquor on our plane." He gave her a lopsided grin. "Though, that could be because at the first sign of any fun, the medical systems alert us to take a shot of correction medication." Before she could again speak, he kissed her. He rocked his hips against her, letting her feel the unmistakable ache of his desire. When he stopped, he held her close. "I've never felt quite like this around any other woman."

He placed his hands on the small of her back, rubbing in circles. Desire wound through her body, unfurling from her stomach. Ariella ran her fingers into his hair. She tasted the sweet tang of liquor on his tongue when they kissed. She wanted him desperately, wanted to feel him inside her. His kisses became aggressive as he nipped at her mouth, drawing her bottom lip between his teeth.

A weight had lifted from her the moment they stepped through the portal and her mood only continued to lighten the longer they stayed in Battlewar Castle. Moaning weakly, she turned her mouth from his and took a deep breath.

"Let's never leave," Ariella whispered. "Let's stay here and make love every night. You can be a lord and I a lady. We'll get a castle. I'll wear tight, corseted dresses. You'll tend to battle wounds and heal scars."

"You have no idea how tempting that is right now." Sebastjan nuzzled her throat, devouring her with deep, passionate kisses. He traced his tongue along her jawline to her ear, where he nipped the lobe. His hard breath resounded in her ear. "You taste sweet."

Her heart beat wildly. Before she realized what was happening, he had her undressed. Sebastjan tossed her clothes aside and began working on his own.

Ariella crawled onto the large bed. The fur tickled in all the right ways. She stretched her arms over her head, lengthening her body. Sebastjan watched with eager eyes. The second his shirt hit the floor, he crawled onto the bed and stretched out next to her.

"Don't move," he said, drawing the back of his hand along the valley of her breasts. His touch whispered over her flesh, sweeping over her stomach and legs, circling her knees, traveling between her parted thighs before making the trip back up her body.

Ariella squirmed restlessly against the bed. Sebastjan moved to settle between her knees. She reached for him, stroking his hair as he placed tiny kisses against her inner thighs.

"So soft and smooth," he said, licking the tender flesh were leg met pussy. Ariella tensed as he blew lightly against the sensitive bud of her sex. He took his time, drawing out the pleasure until she begged him to finish it. He slipped a finger inside her, wiggling and stroking her pussy.

She clutched at his shoulders, pulling him up. He kissed a breast on his way past, before bringing his cock to the slick folds of her sex. A light sheen of sweat covered them, causing the fur to stick to her back. Sebastjan entered her hard and sure. She gasped at the wondrous sensations.

The world seemed to spin around them. Sensations flooded through her, propelled on by the thrusting of their bodies, the soft pants of her voice and the harder grunts of his. Suddenly, she came, tensing as pleasure rippled over her. His release met hers in loud, primitive awareness.

Sebastjan rolled onto the mattress next to her. Ariella watched him close his eyes and take a deep, steadying breath. She placed her hand on his chest to feel the fast beat of his heart and he instantly covered it with his own. She wanted to breathe him in for the rest of her life. She wanted to live in that moment forever, surrounded by the stone of castle walls, light-headed from a combination of drink and sex.

"I think I love you, Ariella," he whispered.

She smiled, watching to see if he'd open his eyes and say more. He didn't, but that didn't lessen her pleasure at his admission. "I think I love you too, Sebastjan."

20

Sebastjan's head throbbed, keeping a steady tempo with his heartbeat. Each thump sent a sharp pain from behind his eyes down the back of his head to his neck. He suddenly appreciated the medical monitoring on his home plane. One shot would cure both his drumming head and his blurred vision.

Ariella looked to be in as much pain as he. She kept her movements to a minimum, often rubbing her temples with the tips of her fingers. With the morning, they both realized it would be impossible to stay in Staria, though Lady Lilith did invite them back for a visit whenever they wanted. Ariella readily agreed and promised to return for the tour of the marketplace.

"Good luck with those hangovers." Lilith chuckled as the blue light from the Starian portal washed over them. This time, as the portal activated, taking them back to his home dimension, he was prepared for the sensation of his body being torn apart. Being prepared didn't help his aching head.

Once back in the Central Hospital, a loud alarm sounded. The familiar smell of the hospital's air filtering sterilizer washed over him, cleaning their bodies and clothes.

"Sterilization commencing," the automated male voice commanded. "Please move away from the platform."

They obeyed. A shield came down, blocking the platform from the scan as a series of lights flashed over them, sweeping them for parasites and viruses from parallel worlds.

"Sterilization complete. Welcome back, Dr. Walter. Welcome back, Sans Ariella. Please move to the orange door."

Instead, Sebastjan went to the wall monitor and brought up Ariella's stats. Studying them, he grinned. "The inter-dimensional travel worked. You're fine. Whatever was in your system is gone now."

Ariella touched her temple. "I wouldn't say fine. I still feel the effects of the drinking sickness."

"That is easily cured. I'll find a syringe we can use." He pulled her with him. "If we hurry, we might be able to get out of here before my father comes to lecture us for not returning yesterday."

21

Ariella wasn't one to press her luck when it came to the Medical Supreme, but even she was a little worried when he didn't seek them out at the hospital and wasn't at home. It wasn't like the man to miss an opportunity to lecture. Was it possible Walter had decided to stay out of Sebastjan and her lives? Somehow, she highly doubted it.

"He probably does not wish to face us before we leave for the research facility," Sebastjan said, tossing her travel bag inside the transport.

"But, you have to admit it is strange." She looked up at the mansion, almost unable to believe she was really free. "It's not like him to run away from a problem."

Sebastjan followed her gaze. "You're right, but

it's just as well. If I saw him, I'd most likely hit him for what he's done. And as much as I hate it, he is Medical Supreme."

"You can't fight the king," Ariella finished for him with an old saying from her homeworld. "He's too powerful. I'm just happy to be getting out of the city with our lives and our health."

"We can't fight him, but we can be a nuisance," Sebastjan said. "This isn't finished."

"I think the best punishment is to never visit, never speak, never transmit to him. He thrives on the attention. Let's not give it to him." Ariella let him help her into the transport.

When he joined her, giving one last glance at the tall mansion, he said, "At least until we have enough evidence against him to do damage. This time he's gone too far."

As the transport door closed, Ariella sighed and settled against her husband. "Can we discuss revenge later? I just want to enjoy—"

"Sebastjan!" A loud knock sounded outside the transport. "Wait!"

"Who is that?" Ariella asked.

Sebastjan reached to open the transport door. "Dr. Lu? What are you doing here?"

"It's your father," Dr. Lu answered.

"What has he done now?" Sebastjan grimaced.

"He's sick," Dr. Lu said. "Something new we haven't seen before. He collapsed soon after you left. Dr. Swift was called back from his ambassadorial duties and has the Medical Supreme isolated in a private care center. We don't want to cause any panic. That's why they sent me to come find you."

Dr. Lu stepped into the transport, nodding once at Ariella before entering new coordinates. Soon they moved through the city streets.

"What's wrong with him?" she asked. "You don't have any idea?"

Dr. Lu opened his mouth, but gave Sebastjan a hesitant look and didn't speak.

"Talk frankly," Sebastjan said. "We both know what my father has done."

Dr. Lu studied Ariella briefly before nodding. "We suspect whatever he had given you, Sans Ariella, has mutated. We've tested the off-plane doctors and all other recent visitors, but they show no signs of the disease. So far, it is contained. Dr. Swift has recommended full lockdown quarantine. That is all I know at this time."

The transport moved through the city toward the edge of town and stopped before a small square building. The place looked like a warehouse unit with plain exterior walls, flat roof and nondescript stone walkway. Dr. Lu glanced around before stepping quickly out onto the quiet street. He lifted his hand to help Ariella down before leading the way into the front door.

Dimly lit pathways were formed between stacks of wooden crates. They were marked with strange symbols she couldn't read. After taking several turns, they finally came to a dead end. Dr. Lu reached for the crate blocking their path and opened it. Inside stairs led down into the floor.

"Where are we going?" she asked.

"The quarantine laboratory," Sebastjan answered. "We cannot risk keeping the Medical Supreme where he will be seen by others. If word spreads that he is sick, and sick with something we have not seen before, people will panic."

"The problem with a medical plane," Dr. Lu interjected, "is that we do not handle the reality of an epidemic well. In theory, we are invaluable as doctors. In practice..." He lifted his hand to the side in a helpless gesture.

"In practice, it has been so long since our world has seen an epidemic that the people tend to panic at the very idea," Sebastjan said. "The concept is practically unheard of."

"We pride ourselves on our health," Dr. Lu added.

"I see," Ariella said, though their admission hardly surprised her.

At the bottom of the stairs, Dr. Lu opened a door. Light streamed in from the laboratory. In the center of the large room the Medical Supreme rested on a bed surrounded by thick plastic. His ashen features were pulled tight, but his eyes remained as sharp as ever. She could feel the displeasure pouring off him. He didn't like being trapped.

Ariella felt a strange sense of power and fear wash over her—power to see him helpless as she'd once been and fear that whatever was happening to him would eventually happen to her. What if she wasn't cured? What if it didn't matter if she was? Would the people of Chiron let her roam free? Or would they lock her up out of fear?

Sebastjan took her arm. "He can't harm you. Nothing will harm you. I promise."

She quickly nodded her head in understanding, believing her husband meant what he said. Whispering, she asked, "What if I have what he has?"

"It would have shown up on your scans when you arrived through the portal," Dr. Lu answered.

"Don't stare at me as if I'm on my deathbed," the

Medical Supreme ordered. "I still have my wits about me."

"That has always been debatable," Sebastjan answered, walking closer to the isolation booth. "I'm assuming you sent for us?"

"You were supposed to be back yesterday," Walter said.

"I will leave you in privacy to speak," Dr. Lu said, walking quickly through the doorway and up the stairs.

"And yet we came back today," Sebastjan said. Ariella felt the tension in his back and felt sorry for him. For all that the Medical Supreme had done, he was still Sebastjan's father. "The great thing about you being in there, Father, is that we don't have to stay and listen to you. So, tell me, what is it you want?"

"Would you speak to me like that if you knew I was dying?" the Medical Supreme demanded.

"You're not dying, at least not yet." Sebastjan walked over to a monitor and began scrolling through the data. "You're just contagious and have to stay in here." Stopping on a screen, he enlarged a photo of a microscopic organism. "They've isolated the abnormality. There is nothing I can do for you."

"You can act in my stead as Medical Supreme

Proxy until I am better. You can live at the mansion while seeing to my duties. You can even fund your precious facility. We'll tell people I have gone on a trip to another plane for medical collection and research and you are training for your future position."

Sebastjan sighed. "No."

"No?" Walter repeated, clearly shocked.

"No," Sebastjan affirmed. "I have told you before. I have no desire to be Medical Supreme."

Walter's pale features filled, becoming flushed. He pushed up on the bed. "Enough of this foolishness. It is your birthright, your duty to be Medical Supreme."

"Did you bring me here to discuss my future or your cure?" Sebastjan inquired. Ariella didn't move as she watched the interplay between the two men. Walter didn't answer. Sebastjan touched the monitor. "I'm sending a copy of the records to my office. If you want my help, you'll send your private records to me as well. I'll help you from my facility. That is all I can do for you."

"That's all you *will* do." Walter fell back on the bed, glaring. "You have always been your mother's son. She too was an ungrateful—"

"Enough!" Ariella yelled. Both men turned to

her, surprised. She gave Sebastjan an apologetic look. To the Medical Supreme, she said, "You are a miserable person. I can honestly say I've never met a more miserable person. That said, the goddesses do not allow me to watch you die. What about taking you through the portal? Will that help?"

"No," Walter said. To her surprise, a snarky comment didn't follow.

"Then there is nothing more we can do for you here," she said. "Your son has offered to work on this problem from his laboratory. Do you want his help?"

For the longest time, the Medical Supreme didn't answer. Then, when she didn't turn her gaze away, he nodded once. The gesture was stiff with anger.

"Very well. Then you will send the files my husband has requested." Ariella moved toward Sebastjan and took his hand. "If you need anything else, perhaps you can find compassion with someone you didn't wrong. But, as you look at these plastic walls, locked away like some tree from the rest of the world, know that the goddesses have laid their justice upon you."

"Goddesses." The Medical Supreme snorted.

"Call it fate, then, if you like," she said. Walter didn't speak again. "Remember me when the insanity of captivity creeps in on you and there is no one you can talk to about it."

"I never locked you up like this," the Medical Supreme said bitterly.

"Gilded bars are still bars," Ariella answered. She saw the light in his eyes darken. There was some grim satisfaction in knowing he was imprisoned by a disease, jailed by his own body and unable to do anything about it. Turning her back on him, she walked away.

Sebastjan finished transmitting the files he needed before making a move to follow his wife. The symmetry of his father's punishment wasn't lost on him, especially since it was done by his own hand.

"Sebastjan," his father said. Sebastjan thought about ignoring him, but something in the man's voice made him stop. "You will work for a cure, won't you? Aside from you, doctors Lu, Swift and Fauchet are the only ones who know. I need you, son."

"I'm not sure you deserve the consideration, but, yes, I will work toward a cure." Sebastjan glanced back to see his father staring at him, the man's eyes pleading. "Unlike you, I would never willingly keep anyone imprisoned if there was something I could do to help. As you said in the past, I take my role as a doctor very seriously."

When he was once more in the transport, Ariella was alone. She said, "Dr. Lu went back to the hospital. Since there is nothing more we can do here, he's wished us well on our trip home."

Sebastjan nodded and began resetting the transport's coordinates. "Part of me wants to let him rot in there."

"You're too good of a man for that." Ariella reached for him, but a light smoke filtered into the transport. Frowning, she covered her mouth and looked as if she would speak. Sebastjan felt his limbs become heavy before his whole world went black.

22

ARIELLA BLINKED, stirring against the thick mattress beneath her body. It took her mind time to focus, but once it did, she shot up on the bed. The smooth walls of the chamber held no decoration, nothing that would set it apart from any other room on dimensional plane 187.

"Hello?" she called only to hear her own voice echo back. "Sebastjan?" Then shivering, she whispered, "Medical Supreme Walter?"

What had Supreme Walter done? Why was she here? Was his illness just a trick to control Sebastjan? And, when it didn't work, did he poison them both with the smoke-filled transport? Dr. Lu had been alone with the unit while the Medical Supreme spoke with them. He would have had time to sabotage their vehicle.

"Sebastjan!" she called louder. Ariella rubbed her arms. Her heartbeat sped and the sudden tension caused her stomach to tighten. What if they'd been separated? What if her words to the Medical Supreme about his own just imprisonment caused him to react to her insolence with a new prison home?

Breathing hard, she went toward the door. It slid open, allowing her out of the room. A long, empty hall with doors lined up on each side stretched before her. She slowly walked toward the end, glancing from side to side.

Touching the smooth, metal wall, she leaned around the corner. The adjoining hall was wider and split into two directions. A couple of doctors with electronic clipboards strode down the hall. They both glanced at her as they passed, but didn't speak and didn't try to stop her.

An arm wound around her waist, jerking her back. She gasped, instantly moving to fight.

"There you are," Sebastjan said. "The computer said your room door had opened and that you were finally awake."

Ariella turned in surprise, hitting his arm. "You

scared me. I thought your father had drugged us and carted me off again."

"The dose must have been too high for you. Everyone else has built an immunity to the sedation." He placed a kiss on the tip of her nose. "I had to carry you to our room—not that I minded."

"What happened exactly? One second, we're getting ready to drive. The next I'm blacking out." Ariella glanced around the empty halls.

"You mean transport sleep?" Sebastjan asked. "It's an automatic transport feature to make long-distance trips more tolerable. But now that I think about it, you might never have had occasion to use it. No wonder you slept so long."

"Where are we?"

"Come. I'll show you." Sebastjan threaded his arm in hers and led her down the hall. "This is my research facility. I know it's not a mansion, but—"

"I don't need a mansion," Ariella assured him. "I'm just happy to be out of the last one I lived in. You could move me to a tiny one-room house for all I care."

"I was going to say, but..." He paused as he reached the end of the hall and swept his hand over a scanner next to a narrow door. As the door slid open, a wave of cool air hit them. It carried the scent of nature and the loud roar of falling water. Yelling, he finished, "But I hope you'll find this place has its charms."

Ariella stepped out onto a balcony platform. A cool mist hit upon her face from a nearby waterfall. She smiled, lifting her hand. The air smelled like air should smell, not sickening sweet with sterilizers. "We're on a different plane, aren't we? The trees aren't behind windows."

"No, we're in a perception room." He lifted his hand to the wall. The waterfall and balcony disappeared, replaced by metal grate floors and walls. "We're helping to test them before they're offered to the population. The technology was traded though the Divinity portal. We call them relaxation retreats. I thought, perhaps, you might want to work with a couple of the developers to maybe make a scene from your home world. We could use the input of someone who wasn't born here. Several of the scientists keep trying to change the smell of the air."

Ariella nearly teared up at the thoughtfulness of the gesture. She nodded. "Yes, I would love to recreate my home world very much."

Sebastjan pulled her close to him. "You know, I meant what I said on Staria. I was not suffering from the drinking sickness."

"The part where you said you think you love me?" Ariella asked.

"I know I love you."

"I love you too, Sebastjan." Ariella leaned into his embrace. "Are there security monitors in here?"

"Yes." Frowning, he glanced around. "Why?"

"Can you turn them off?"

"Yes." A slow smile curled on his mouth and lit in his eyes.

"Then lock the door and make the waterfall come back." She pulled his face to hers. "I want to show you just how in love with you I am."

The End

THE SERIES CONTINUES...

See what happens on plane 187 in the next Divinity Healers series installment

Seducing Cecilia
(Divinity Healers 2)
by Michelle M. Pillow

In a world obsessed with medical advancement, Dr. Gerard Fauchet longs for something more. When he's assigned as the liaison to an off-plane dignitary, he never imagined she'd be so stunningly beautiful, or so damned frustrating. One second she's kissing him, the next she's pretending nothing is between them. The passion is scorching, everything he ever dreamed of having with a woman. He'll make her admit she wants him—or die trying.

Dr. Cecilia Markos is keenly aware that she's been shoved through a portal to an alternate reality for one reason—to bring home medical advancements for the betterment of her people. Unfortunately, she only has two months to learn a world's complete medical knowledgebase. It's an impossible task made even more so by the distractingly handsome Gerard who she can't seem to keep her hands or her mind off of.

As the clash heats up between Gerard and Cecilia, the clock is ticking, and the time for seduction is running out.

A first look at Chapter One!

City of Asclepius, Country of Chiron, Dimensional Plane 187

Dr. Gerard Fauchet tried to hide the spark of jealousy he felt when he looked at his childhood friend, Dr. Sebastjan Walter. Sebastjan nodded politely as his father's guests moved through the receiving line to congratulate him on his new marriage. The son of the Medical Supreme, Sebastjan had lived an easy life. His family had money, position and political power. Medical Supreme Walter was easily the highest ranking official on the planet and he was in charge of allotting all of the planet's medical research funding. To a world obsessed with medical advancements, research funding was like air and bodily sustenance.

Gerard focused his attention on his friend. It wasn't Sebastjan's birthright or money or power or position that made the pang of jealous filter over Gerard. It was Sebastjan's new wife—Ariella. A true, exotic beauty, Ariella came from an alternate dimension of reality. Ever since Gerard heard about inter-dimensional plane travel, he'd become obsessed thinking about it. He never really wanted to be a doctor. It was just what everyone on his plane had to become. He much rather spend his days reading and learning about culture and history than studying one of the over abundantly available medical books that filled every home and office.

Like most nice homes in Asclepius, the front room of Supreme Walter's mansion was overly sterile, each surface hard and unwelcoming but for a few engraved curls and wisps decorating the borders.

Marble and metal blended together with great square columns to form self-sterilizing walls. However, the Medical Supreme did have a vast array of items collected from other parallel universes. Gerard found himself staring at them, wondering about those other worlds. What kinds of places were they to dedicate so much time to books that told unreal stories and to creating things of elegance and beauty for the mere sake of elegance and beauty?

When he looked at Ariella, he thought of all the things she knew—non-medical things, small facts that would mean nothing to her but would provide endless fascination for him. The women on his plane talked like doctors, thought like doctors, were mostly doctors. Not Ariella. She was a Sans, a non-doctor. Sans Ariella. And the very idea of her captivated him.

"Dr. Fauchet, how good of you to come," Sebastjan said.

"How could I not?" Gerard answered his friend. The loneliness that welled within him as he looked at Ariella became almost unbearable, so he hid it behind a playful smile and flirtatious wink.

"Couldn't miss my reception?" Sebastjan asked, skeptical.

"I couldn't miss the Medical Supreme's

summons," Gerard corrected. "You didn't think everyone was here to see you, did you?"

Ariella gave a short burst of laughter at the insolent joke.

Gerard winked at her but continued talking to Sebastjan. "Apparently, I am to host two off-plane dignitaries coming here to learn our secrets. However," he turned his full attention to Ariella, "while I am here…"

He wasn't a fool. All the thoughts running through his head would never come to fruition. Though he found her very pretty, he didn't know her, not really. He would leave the mansion and perhaps only cross path with her a handful more times in his life. Her tiny secrets would remain hers as she lived out her days as a doctor's wife.

"Sans Ariella," Sebastjan introduced, "my childhood playmate and local lawbreaker—"

"That is distinguished gentleman and dignitary host," Gerard corrected.

"Dr. Gerard Fauchet," Sebastjan finished.

"A great pleasure," Gerard said, his playful eyes studying Ariella's face. "And it was only one tiny law fourteen years ago. There was a medication mishap, it was hot and it was only the male chairmen who complained about my nakedness. I swear I am a reformed man." Sebastjan cleared his throat. Gerard laughed, not showing a single second of remorse at having been caught flirting with the new bride. Leaning into Ariella, he whispered, "An even greater pleasure to see you've managed to make Sebastjan jealous over you."

Ariella blushed. Sebastjan frowned at them. Gerard bowed his head and moved on.

"What? No present?" Sebastjan mumbled after him. Gerard laughed, but didn't turn back around.

New Order Society, Dimensional Plane 303

Dr. Cecilia Markos stared at her foot, absently following the lines of her citizen number with her eyes. "One. Zero. Eight. Seven. Five." She didn't need to read it to know it. The tight, neat script had been inked into her flesh the day she was born. It concealed the new implants the government instated as an enhancement to the anti-chaos movement.

One. Zero. Eight. Seven. Five.

Those numbers were everything—her money access, her doctor credentials, her purchasing rations, her identification. Everyone living in the New Order

Society had a designation. It was the only way a society could thrive. There had to be order to chaos.

It seemed strange then, that she would be going to a place where those numbers meant nothing. A tiny shiver of fear washed over her. A few months ago, she'd never dreamt that visiting an alternate universe was possible. Now, she was to be one of two women going to a new world—another plane of existence, another reality, their world but not their world.

An entity called Divinity Corporation had mastered the science of inter-dimensional travel and, two years ago, they had made contact with Cecelia's plane. Already a few of her people had gone through the portal gates to new dimensions. When Politician Shinclus first approached her, she'd thought he'd needed medical attention. The existence of the portals weren't common knowledge amongst her people. But, she'd since seen it for herself. She watched as people appeared out of nothing, carrying strange objects traded from other realms.

A few short months and so much had changed. All the waiting and planning, reading and studying, worrying and pretending not to worry had all led to this day. Today, she would be traveling to an alternate reality.

The New Order Society plane was only one of

four-hundred-thirty-six mapped dimensions used by Divinity—each as different as the last. Some had vampires and werewolves, some had faeries and gnomes, and some had humanoids so alien her dimension's species were hardly compatible. Many of them, like hers, had never even heard of dimensional travel or portals. Some societies were obsessed to the point of compulsion and some so brutal they enjoyed watching gladiators fight to the death. One thing many of them seemed to have in common was chaos. Utter, uncontrolled chaos. New Order Society thrived on anti-chaos—no unconformity, no inappropriate behaviors, and absolutely no crime.

Looking at an alternate reality was supposed to be like seeing your world had history changed. There were many similarities. Languages were relatively similar. Some people had the same appearance, but were not the same people. Certain events like natural disasters could be shared. People were human-like in appearance and functions, though she had been told of a race of people that didn't have toenails.

Cecilia wiggled her toes, wondering what they'd look like without nails. Then, sighing, she stood and reached for her best one piece suit. Red material belled around the legs and led up to tightly-fitted hips and a looser bodice. The sleeves were long, falling past her hands. She brushed her hair back from her face, trying not to think about the fashionable crimson red streak she'd been forced to get rid of. Apparently, this medical plane she was going to didn't have the same fashions. In New Order Society everyone sported a bright streak of color in their hair. Just because they were orderly didn't mean they couldn't be fun, too. Well, that and the streak proved the wearer had been to their mandatory grooming appointment by the lack of a line of demarcation where the new growth came in.

Taking a deep breath, Cecilia pulled on her boots, whispering, "It's only for a couple of months. It will be fine. It's only a couple of months. I'll be able to make it back. Everyone else has made it back home."

Despite her words, she wasn't so sure.

**For more information, visit
www.MichellePillow.com**

***New York Times* & *USA TODAY*
Bestselling Author**

Michelle loves to travel and try new things, whether it's a paranormal investigation of an old Vaudeville Theatre or climbing Mayan temples in Belize. She believes life is an adventure fueled by copious amounts of coffee.

Newly relocated to the American South, Michelle is involved in various film and documentary projects with her talented director husband. She is mom to a fantastic artist. And she's managed by a dog and cat who make sure she's meeting her deadlines.

For the most part she can be found wearing pajama pants and working in her office. There may or may not be dancing. It's all part of the creative process.

Come say hello! Michelle loves talking with readers on social media!

www.MichellePillow.com

facebook.com/AuthorMichellePillow

twitter.com/michellepillow

instagram.com/michellempillow

bookbub.com/authors/michelle-m-pillow

goodreads.com/Michelle_Pillow

amazon.com/author/michellepillow

youtube.com/michellepillow

pinterest.com/michellepillow

COMPLIMENTARY EXCERPTS

TRY BEFORE YOU BUY!

LINNEA'S ARRANGEMENT

DIVINITY HEALERS BOOK THREE

Alternate Reality Romance, Part of the Divinity Universe

Beautiful, highly intelligent Linnea Nel wants what most women want—a career, love, respect. But coming from a plane where order and all things anti-chaos reign, the untrackable, untraceable and highly rebellious Linnea is considered a threat—to her family, society and her world. When her numerous arrests for reading library books become a public embarrassment to her politically minded sister, Linnea is forced on a dignitary mission to an alternate reality.

There are only two classifications of people on plane 187: Doctors and Not Doctors (Sans). Dr. Sam

Swift is one of the highest ranking officials on the medical plane, answering only to the Medical Supreme. When the Medical Supreme becomes ill, it's up to him to find a cure. Nowhere in this equation is there room—or time—to fall in love. And then he meets the exquisitely frustrating Sans Linnea Nel.

In the midst of the worst outbreak 187's society has faced in decades, two people who never should have met fall in love. How can Linnea stay where she may be in danger? But how can Sam let the love of his life go?

Chapter One Excerpt

NEW ORDER SOCIETY, DIMENSIONAL PLANE 303

Linnea Nel eyed the bars of her cell. The New Order Society government wouldn't keep her locked up long. They never did. For every second she stayed in jail, the higher her offender ranking number would go. Since all number statistics were reported to the public, they would prefer she was ranked as a misdemeanor disturbance as opposed to anything major—like thievery or, worse, public chaos.

As one of the few people whose body's natural magnetism didn't allow for the anti-chaos implant, she was on every government and societal watch list. As a child, she'd managed to blend. Linnea had been a good student, a model participant in societal functions. Then came graduation. No higher learning institutes would take her. They didn't even bother to give her a good reason why she was rejected. Without an implant, they had no way of ensuring she did her own coursework and followed institutional policies. So it didn't matter how good she was or how smart. Unlike all other students, she would never be under their complete monitoring and control. They couldn't risk putting her into a position of power. They couldn't risk educating her. So she'd educated herself.

"Come on out of there, Nel," Orderkeeper Delkin said. The man should have instilled fear in her with his Goliath size, but Linnea had been in his cell way too many times. "And don't let us catch you in the library again without permission."

"Wouldn't dream of it," she answered dryly.

"Yeah," he muttered. "You know what to do.

When you're checked out of the system, there's some people here waiting to talk to you."

People? Linnea frowned. Her own parents barely spoke to her—the uncontrollable one. Since she moved into New Order City, they hadn't really spoken to her. Why should they when her older brother and sister both did the family proud? Her genetic fluke only caused them embarrassment. To society's way of thinking, since she couldn't be watched, she was destined to cause trouble. She'd stopped trying to impress her parents years ago. Some battles couldn't be won, so there was no point in fighting them.

"See you next time around, keeper." Linnea typed in her identification number and made her way toward the front of the Orderkeeper Station. The tracking monitors made a familiar beep as she was scanned and found without a chip. They had tried making her wear a few around her neck, but her body's natural energy made them glitch. Once the monitor even read her as the wrong person—a dead singer, to be precise. That little event had raised a lot of alarms. There were still rumors that Silev had faked his own death and was really alive. What could she say? Diehard fans would believe anything. The only reason the orderkeepers didn't lock her up was because the authorities were fearful word of her condition would get out. Societal control depended on society trusting the implants implicitly.

"Linnea."

Linnea paused by the open door and slowly moved to stand in the doorway. Out of all the people who'd come to the station to get her, she never expected to see her sister. When they were little, Jinna had been her best friend. Now, looking at the woman, she couldn't see that little girl. Instead, she saw the pristine and orderly countenance of Politician Nel, new leader of the anti-chaotic task force.

"Jin," Linnea answered. Like everyone else on the planet, her sister wore the one-piece suit. Material that belled around the legs led to tightly-fitted hips and a looser bodice. Her black hair had been streaked along the side with a bright, unnatural red, and tiny jewels had been adhered in a swirl pattern along the inside of it.

Linnea preferred to keep her black hair shorter with a streak of dark purple to match the purplish grey of her eyes. Her bodice was tight, less conservative in design. A thick, black belt wrapped her ribs, dark purple over black material.

"Leave us," Jinna ordered her two guards.

Linnea didn't back away as they passed, even as they stared at her like she was about to attack her own sister.

When they were alone, Linnea stepped into the room.

"This needs to stop," Jinna said. "I can't have a sister who's constantly being arrested for petty chaotic crimes."

"I'm great, thanks for asking, Jin," Linnea answered, moving to the long bench next to the wall. She took a seat and stretched her feet forward in easy repose. Smiling pleasantly, though she hardly felt pleasant, she inquired, "And you?"

"Always a child." Jinna frowned.

"Ah, Jin, I think you're being too hard on yourself. You've done well. I wouldn't call you a child." Linnea smirked. The look was a mask, a way of keeping the true depths of her hurt to herself. She wanted so badly to live a normal life, to have a family, find love and marry, have a career and a well-earned respect. Instead, she was arrested for daring to better herself.

"I didn't mean me," Jinna answered, flustered. "You are always a child. This proves my point. Do you ever think of anyone but yourself?"

Dropping all pretenses, Linnea drew her feet in

and placed her elbows on her knees. "I was reading a book, not running naked through the streets."

"Not this time," Jinna grumbled.

"Once. I ran naked through the streets once. I was angry. You would be too if your application to medical learning was denied because of a stupid inability to take an implant. My grades were better than yours. I passed all my tests. I had recommendations and—"

"I'm not here to debate the past," Jinna interrupted.

"It's not the past," Linnea said. "It's my present, my future." She leaned over, jerking off her boot to expose her bare foot. A black numbered tattoo stared back at them, her identification number. Normally, the implants would be placed underneath the visible mark. Those numbers were everything—her money access, her education and work history, her purchasing rations, her identification. Everyone living in the New Order Society had a designation. When they were children, the government trucks had visited their school. The technicians wore costumes as to not frighten them. They danced and sang as the coded implants were injected beneath every child's number. Linnea's body rejected the implant, and every one after that.

Her scarred foot attested to it. "It's not like I'm unwilling to be part of the system. I almost lost my foot to infection because I had the damned chip implanted too many times. I know the law. I know that this is the only way society can thrive. There must be order to chaos. You all just won't let me be a part of your society! It's not like I can help some natural electrical magnetism in my body—a current your doctors can't even define. Maybe if you let me go to school I could figure it out. I could design a better implant."

"Funding will not be granted to cure one person, Linnea. The needs of the many will be met first."

"The needs of the many? Like using chemists to make better-smelling grooming products?" Linnea wanted to scream, but knew that would do no good. "I could do that too."

"I'm here to discuss your future." When Jinna looked at her, Linnea didn't feel as if her sister actually saw her.

"You're letting me go to school?" Hope filled her.

"You know I can't do that."

The hope died. Though she should have been used to it by now, the disappointment physically hurt. "Then what?"

"I've secured a position for you with Dr. Cecilia

Markos as an assistant." Jinna smiled for the first time.

"Assistant?"

"Don't look so disappointed. You clearly want to be in the medical field since you're constantly sneaking into the library to read medical textbooks."

"I read fiction too," Linnea said, just to be contrary. "Perhaps I really dream of being make-believe."

Even as part of her wanted to jump at the chance to be near medicine, another part knew that to be merely an assistant would eventually wear her down. To be so close and not be able to succeed. It would be torture.

"Dr. Cecilia Markos is fast becoming one of our greatest assets. You're lucky she's willing to take you with her."

"With her?" Linnea stood. "Where? Are you banishing me? New Order City is my home."

"Dr. Markos has been assigned to the off-plane program. You will be joining her on a trip through what we call the Divinity portal to a medically advanced dimensional plane in a parallel universe. It's primarily an ambassadorial journey, a basic trading of goodwill while gauging the plane's medical knowledge and their usefulness to our world."

"Portal travel?" Linnea felt a shiver work over her body. "I was joking when I said I wanted to be make-believe."

"When have you ever known me to joke?" Jinna arched a brow.

Good point.

"What do you mean a portal to a parallel universe?" she asked.

"Exactly that. You're smart, so I know I don't have to explain the concept of alternate realities and parallel universes to you. So take the theories you know and suppose they are real. Suppose someone found a way to move between the veils, so to speak. Looking at an alternate reality is like seeing our world if history had been altered in some way. Languages are similar, so you will not have a problem in that department. I'm told some people will look the same, but do not mistake them for being the same people. Humans will look like humans, save a few minor differences."

Linnea opened her mouth to speak, but said nothing. Jinna was serious.

"An entity called Divinity Corporation mastered the science of inter-dimensional travel. About two years ago they made contact with us. Since then, we've allowed a portal gate to be placed on our world.

We're one of four-hundred-thirty-six charted universes, with infinitely more out there. We plan on staking a big claim in Divinity's project. Several ambassadors have been sent through and have come back successfully. Dr. Markos will lead the medical team. You will be her assistant."

Linnea frowned. "Team?"

"Well, a team of two. You and her."

"Why haven't I heard of this?"

"And cause societal panic? No. The public will not be made aware of these developments. There is no need to concern them. The government knows what is best for them."

"What if I say no? What if I tell? Your secret would be out."

Jinna laughed. "Do you still believe you can make people listen to you? Lin, Lin, Lin." Jinna shook her head in amusement. "You don't have a choice. You're going. It's what is best for societal harmony. I'm sure you understand."

"And when it's over? When I come back?" Linnea stiffened, a strange feeling of dread unfurling inside her. But, this was her sister. She didn't want to believe that Jinna would do something to hurt her.

"Why don't you concentrate your efforts on dealing with today? My guards have the information you need." Jinna left, leaving Linnea to stare after her. No matter how fantastic her sister's words were, Linnea found the idea of an alternate reality easier to believe than Jinna actually teasing her with this ridiculous conversation.

LILITH ENRAPTURED
DIVINITY WARRIORS 1

Alternate Reality Romance

Sorin of Firewall lives in a land forever at war. In fact, the Starian men are so busy fighting, their marriage ceremony has been reduced to a "will of the gods" event where they simply pick a woman out of a lineup and claim her as a wife. With women becoming scarce, it's necessary to trade the offworld Divinity Corporation for brides. Duty-bound to attend the ceremony, he has no intention of picking a bride, let alone one from another dimension. That is, until he sees Lilith, the bewitching woman sent by the gods to reward—or punish?—him.

For a complete, up-to-date booklist, visit www.MichellePillow.com

THE DRAGON'S QUEEN
BY MICHELLE M. PILLOW

Dragon Lords Series

Bestselling Shapeshifter Romance

Mede of the Draig knows three things for a fact: As the only female dragon shifter of her people, she is special. She can kick the backside of any man. And she absolutely doesn't want to marry.

Mede has spent a lifetime trying to prove herself as strong as any male warrior. Unfortunately, being the special, rare creature she is, she's been claimed as the future bride to nearly three dozen Draig—each one confident that when they come for her hand in marriage fate will choose them. When the men aren't bragging about how they're going to marry her, they're acting like she's a delicate rare flower in need of their protection.

She is far from a shrinking solarflower.

Prince Llyr of the Draig knows four things for a fact: He is the future king of the dragon shifters. He must act honorably in all ways. He absolutely, positively is meant to marry Lady Mede. And she dead set against marriage.

Llyr's fate rests in the hands of a woman determined not to have any man. With a new threat emerging amongst their cat shifting neighbors, a threat whose eyes are focused firmly on Mede, time may be running out. It is up to him to convince her to be his dragon queen.

The Dragon's Queen Excerpt

There were three things Medellyn knew for a fact. She was special. She could kick the ass of any boy. And she did not want to marry and have babies.

She was special.

Medellyn was one of the only dragon shifting females in all the universe, and definitely in all of the

Draig. Only once in a thousand births was a female dragon shifter born. She was rare, or so everyone kept telling her. Her childhood was a strange contradiction. Her very proper mother tried to treat her as if she were some sacred crystal that might crack. Her warrior father tried to make her train like a boy while dressing like a girl.

She could kick the ass of any boy.

Medellyn hated when boys tried to act as if she were weak and to be protected. Her dragon was just as fierce as any of theirs, probably more so. To prove her point, she'd gladly pummel any who had challenged her to the ground...and some who hadn't.

She *absolutely, positively* did not want to marry and have babies.

Being the special, rare creature she was, in the twenty not-so-sweet girlhood years of her life she'd been claimed as the future bride to nearly three dozen boys—each one confident that when they came of the age to marry she would make their crystals glow and they hers.

Glowing crystals wasn't just a metaphor. On the day she was born, her father journeyed to Crystal Lake like all the new fathers did. He dove beneath the waves, swam down to the deepest part and pulled her stone from the lakebed. Like all Draig children, she wore the stone around her neck, and would continue to wear it until the day it glowed telling her which of the dragon shifting men she was destined by the gods to marry. Okay, technically she might be destined to marry an offworlder like most Draig men, but no one on her planet seemed to think so.

Gods bones, she hoped she wasn't destined to end up with any of the idiots on her planet. They had yet to impress her.

When it was her turn to go to the Breeding Festival, the crystal would glow signifying her *curse* for all to see. Well, her "blessing" as her mother called it. Lady Grace did not appreciate her daughter calling marriage a curse. Grace did not appreciate a lot of things that Medellyn liked, such as swords and bows, ceffyl riding, camping alone in the forest, hunting, sparring, smashing arrogant looks off of dragon men's faces.

It was a fight with her mother that sent her running through the mountain forest. Medellyn hated the woman, hated what her mother wanted her daughter to be. Grace was only a human, brought to their planet as a bartered bride. She married Medellyn's father without question and spent most of her days completely in docile agreement with whatever her husband said. Medellyn couldn't imagine taking anyone else's opinions over her own.

Her father, Axell, was a highly praised warrior in the Draig army and carried the title of Top Breeder of the ceffyls. The man's whole life focused on four things: his wife, his only child, and mares and steeds. Her father was a very important man, but his work kept him away from home several nights a week as he slept outdoors with the herd. With a three-year gestation period and only about fifty percent live-birth rate, the animals were not a resource that could be easily renewed. His ceffyls supplied the soldiers with mounts and farmers used them for beasts of burden to help with the fields.

Like Axell, Medellyn was a proud dragon. Had she been born male, she would have been a warrior, too. Instead, she was *special*. How could her human mother begin to understand the wildness than ran in her dragon blood? If she had, Grace would never have asked Medellyn to tame her spirit.

Breathing hard, she came to an abrupt halt and screamed into the trees. Her body shook with rage and she tore at the pretty gown she wore. She hated her body, hated being special, hated being expected to act like a lady when she felt like a dragon. Her taloned finger snagged on the crystal around her neck and she cut the leather strap of the necklace. The crystal flew several feet away.

"I am not some man's chattel," she yelled, knowing she'd run far enough away that her mother could not hear her retorts. Since she was shifted her voice was hoarse and powerful, and she reveled in the fierceness of it. "I am not some breeding ceffyl to have children. It is not my place to give you fifty grandkids. I can't help you only had one child. If you would have made me a boy, I wouldn't be a disappointment to you!"

Tears stung her eyes as Medellyn walked aimlessly, searching the forest floor for the fallen necklace. Finding it, she grabbed the inert crystal into her fist. It was a reminder of all she was expected to be. She took a deep breath, looking at her fist and then to the stones littering the forest floor. A small smile formed on her mouth. Medellyn dropped the crystal on the hard ground and glared at it. Rage boiled inside her, the kind of rage surely only a dragon shifter could feel.

"This is what I think of your fate," she growled as she fell to her knees.

Medellyn grabbed a heavy rock and smashed it down onto her necklace. The crystal cracked. The noise gave her some satisfaction so she hit it again.

Grunting with each strike of the stone, she didn't stop until her future had been ground to dust.

"That is what I think of your destiny."

To find out more about Michelle's books visit MichellePillow.com